What the critics are saying…

"An intriguing journey into an unknown world... characters are strong and proud, but also, tragic and sad." ~ *Ecartaromance review.*

"A story of love, hardship and rewards. One you'll want to hurry through the first time because of the fluidity of the writing and the visuals of the unfolding story. You'll read it again for the nuances." ~ *Romance Junkies*

"Intriguing characters with well developed personalities... Sex senses are hotter than a roaring campfire and very well detailed. A tale of love and lust in a primitive society." ~ *Coffee Time Romance.*

Vonna Harper

Captive Warrior

Ellora's Cave
Romantica Publishing

An Ellora's Cave Romantica Publication

www.ellorascave.com

Captive Warrior

ISBN # 1419952528
ALL RIGHTS RESERVED.
Captive Warrior Copyright© 2005 Vonna Harper
Edited by: Sue-Ellen Gower
Cover art by: Syneca

Electronic book Publication: March, 2005
Trade paperback Publication: September, 2005

Excerpt from *Scarlet Cavern* Copyright © Vonna Harper, 2004

With the exception of quotes used in reviews, this book may not be reproduced or used in whole or in part by any means existing without written permission from the publisher, Ellora's Cave Publishing, Inc.® 1056 Home Avenue, Akron OH 44310-3502.

This book is a work of fiction and any resemblance to persons, living or dead, or places, events or locales is purely coincidental. The characters are productions of the authors' imagination and used fictitiously.

Warning:

The following material contains graphic sexual content meant for mature readers. *Captive Warrior* has been rated *E-rotic* by a minimum of three independent reviewers.

Ellora's Cave Publishing offers three levels of Romantica™ reading entertainment: S (S-ensuous), E (E-rotic), and X (X-treme).

S-*ensuous* love scenes are explicit and leave nothing to the imagination.

E-*rotic* love scenes are explicit, leave nothing to the imagination, and are high in volume per the overall word count. In addition, some E-rated titles might contain fantasy material that some readers find objectionable, such as bondage, submission, same sex encounters, forced seductions, etc. E-rated titles are the most graphic titles we carry; it is common, for instance, for an author to use words such as "fucking", "cock", "pussy", etc., within their work of literature.

X-*treme* titles differ from E-rated titles only in plot premise and storyline execution. Unlike E-rated titles, stories designated with the letter X tend to contain controversial subject matter not for the faint of heart.

Also by Vonna Harper:

Dangerous Ride
Dark Touch
Equinox anthology
Equinox II anthology
Forced
Hard Bodies
Her Passionate Need
More Than Skin Deep anthology
Refuge
Scarlet Cavern
Storm Warnings anthology
Thunder

Captive Warrior

Chapter One

"You are ready?"

The Sakar woman-warrior, Nuwaa, pulled her abuli bone sword from its leather sheath, but although she knew and accepted what was expected of her, she continued to hold the weapon in a hand made strong by seasons of preparation and battle. The sword, fashioned from the rib of the dangerous meat-eater, represented her position within the clan. If the order hadn't come from her liege-lord, she would never surrender it.

"Yes," she said at length. Feeling the loss, she handed the sword to the aging but still-powerful man who ruled the two hundred-strong clan with a mix of confidence, intellect, and responsibility.

"You hesitate," Liege-lord Radislay said with a short nod. "Good. To a woman-warrior, her weapons are life. Now your knife."

Careful to keep her expression neutral, Nuwaa did as commanded. Not sure what to expect next, but well-trained in dedication and obedience, she settled her arms at her sides. Liege-lord Radislay crossed his arms over his muscular chest and regarded her from beneath white lashes. To be singled out from the tribe's other warriors filled her with pride and a measure of concern she'd never reveal. What if she didn't live up to her ruler's expectations? After everything he and the other councilmen had said about the need to cut off the head of their enemy, the Kebo, what if he'd decided she wasn't worthy after all? *No!* She *would* succeed! She had to. Her clan's safety and continued existence depended on it.

"The Kebo are less than animals," Radislay said as his serpentine green eyes licked like fire over her body. "To them women have no use beyond spreading their legs. Haddard, the creature they call their liege-lord, will want you. One look at you—enemy and female with eyes and hair like midnight and a body made for mating—and nothing will satisfy him except having you roped and on your knees before him, his slave in every way."

"Haddard?" The idea of being any man's slave-whore, like the prospect of failure in battle, weakened a warrior. She would *not* let herself be touched with the possibility. "Liege-lord, please tell me more about him."

Radislay was a soul-deep leader. He feared nothing and put his people's safety and prosperity above his own life. When he was younger and a fighter, he was never wounded or taken prisoner. He'd killed many enemy and some of their skulls rested on the great stone piles outside his *mogan*. But as she watched his expression darken, she wondered if, somehow, her liege feared this enemy in ways he never had before.

"You have already heard what you must, that the creature who believes himself worthy of leading the savage Kebo, directs his war-lieges to attack all who dare resist their raids. For many seasons the Kebo roamed far from here, and I believed we were safe, but he has grown brave and vengeful." Radislay's voice dropped. "It is as I have long thought, revenge rules him."

"Revenge? For what?"

Looking sober, Radislay waved off her question. "Haddard lives for the letting of enemy blood, particularly mine. He has no heart and is a belly-dragging animal. His war-lieges are animals themselves—cougars and wolves and abuli, tearers of living flesh."

She'd been raised and trained to fight the cougars, wolves, and abuli of enemy tribes. As a consequence, she ached to bury her sharp blades in Kebo flesh before they could do the same to her and her fellow clansmen.

"I will kill him before he or his touch our most precious tribe members, our breeder-women. Whatever you command my liege, I will do it."

She extended her fighting hand toward her weapons but instead of returning them to her, her liege shook his head. "Did you not hear me, Nuwaa? Yes, you will battle and win but not in ways you have ever done before. Your value to your people comes from your unique ability to be brought close to Haddard, not by killing."

"I do not understand."

"Not yet but you soon will. Earlier during the warrior-gathering, I made clear why we must attack the Kebo instead of simply protecting ourselves against the invaders as other tribes do. Other clans believe they will survive because they fortify their villages and keep guards out at all times. But I know Haddard and his thinking all too well. Nothing means more to him than shedding Sakar blood, my blood."

Wondering what had caused the change in tone, Nuwaa waited for her liege to continue. "Haddard and the Kebo attack because they are aggressors. They will not expect the Sakar to do the same, which is why they will not be ready for us. Our warriors will kill many of the enemy, but Haddard will not be among them."

Her liege had already explained that Haddard remained with the rest of his clan when his warriors attacked so no matter what happened in battle, he could rule. His life meant the Kebo would continue to live and prosper.

"You will fight well," Radislay continued. "I have watched you for many seasons. I know your fierce, brave nature. But even bravery and countless prayers to your spirit cannot ensure that an enemy weapon will not find you."

"I know." *I accept what my spirit decides.*

"If you are killed, your people will always remember and honor you. But hopefully you will be captured."

Hopefully? Bile rose in her throat. Like the rest of the Sakar warriors, she hated the thought of helplessness more than she feared what an enemy might do to her.

"Nuwaa, you are here alone with me because I have a plan only you can fulfill."

Her heart rate increased. Pride swelled her chest. "I am honored."

"I knew you would be. Nuwaa, I want you to be captured."

"What?"

Radislay's attention slid from her to the weapons he held. "It must happen! All those the Kebo capture are brought to Haddard. And when he sees you, he will not cut off your head but keep you."

"I would rather be dead!"

"So speaks a warrior. But listen to me." He leaned closer. "Think of your position as his hostage. By staying at his side, submitting to his animal needs, doing whatever he commands of you, you will learn his secrets and weaknesses."

"I am not a slave-whore." She ground out the word given to the pathetic creatures who traveled with armies much as hyenas and vultures followed plant-eating herds. "I am spirit and strength, not soft flesh."

"No," her liege said with his gaze fixed on the space between her legs barely covered by the soft thigh-length skirt made of tightly woven reeds and fiber. All that stood between her and nudity was the practical skirt and waist-length sleeveless shirt which tied over one shoulder, covered her breasts, and dipped under the opposite arm. Although sturdy, the material was loose to allow for freedom of movement.

"No," Radislay repeated. "You are not a slave-whore, but Haddard will want to make you his." Without asking permission, something he didn't have to do because he commanded every aspect of his warriors' lives and bodies, he grabbed her top and lifted it, exposing her breasts. "You are blessed," he said as he flicked a nipple. "Your body is a gift from Lifelight."

Lifelight was God among gods, the mystical being who lived in the sun and provided the Sakar with a lush world to live and prosper in. "I do not deserve to be called His gift," she said as Radislay caught her nipples between thumb and forefinger. "I do not know my origin. I do not remember my mother."

"Perhaps you did not have one. What Lifelight creates comes from his hands and breath. Look at what sets you apart from most. Your hair and eyes are black, your flesh deep and rich-colored. Certainly Lifelight blessed you."

She needed to concentrate on what he was saying, to try to decide whether he might be right, but his fingers on her breasts distracted her. She'd fucked and been fucked countless times. Warriors took of each other whenever they wanted. Although the couplings merged in her mind, she doubted she'd ever be able to control her body's response. Older women-warriors had told her that the seasons would quiet the fire between her legs, but she wasn't sure, or that she'd want it. Yes, the fire served as proof of her human weakness, her lack of command over this one aspect of her life, but she loved the explosion of heat and the growing flames that preceded release.

"Haddard will see these—" he rolled her nipples between his fingers, "—and know no rest until he believes they, and you, belong to him."

"If he touches me—" She took a deep breath that didn't calm her as much as she needed. "I will choke the life from him."

"No." Her liege slapped a breast. "You will not. Not until you have learned his secrets and plans, but most of all, the Kebo's weakness." He smiled. "Then make his blood flow. Bathe yourself in it and bring me back his head."

"I live for that moment."

Radislay continued to lay claim to her breasts. She waited, caught somewhere between anticipation and uncertainty because her liege had a lifemate and his days of sharing and being shared were behind him. She couldn't imagine he wanted her to spread her legs for him. Instead, this foreplay must have a different purpose.

"You like to fuck, do you not?" he asked. They'd been standing in the middle of the large *mogan* used for meetings and other gatherings. When he suddenly pushed her so hard she nearly lost her balance, she backed up. He kept after her, pressing her breasts until she'd backed all the way to the rough-finished wooden wall. "My warriors tell me you can take a cock in your mouth and make a man believe he is going to die."

"Men boast." Instinct told her to resist, but she forced herself to keep her hands off her liege.

Radislay smiled, the grin caught by the lit torches that ringed the room. "They do. I know not to believe everything they say, but when over and over again I hear the same thing, I believe." He continued to keep a hand hard against a breast. At the same time, he pushed her skirt up around her waist, revealing her core. "You fuck willingly whenever the time and your need is right, do you not?"

"Yes."

"Always willingly?"

"I do not understand."

"You will. This is what today is about." He slid first one and then two fingers into the opening between her legs. Although surprised, she widened her stance. He was, after all, her liege-lord. He increased the penetration. As he did, his breathing quickened. Perhaps reacting to his excitement, she felt the first heat touch her. He continued his exploration. She tried to imagine herself truly fucking him but they would never be equals. She revered this man she considered a near god and had never dreamed of laying with him. Still, her body heard its own song and responded to the music that lived deep inside her.

"Wet already." He withdrew his fingers and wiped them on her belly. "Quick to heat. But what if sex was forced on you, part of being captured? What would happen then?"

"I do not know." Her belly tightened, and her throat felt hot. She hadn't experienced such nervousness since her first uncertain days as a woman-warrior.

"We must find out."

For a moment he did nothing more than study her. Although she was accustomed to being stared at, his intense gaze reminded her of what set her apart from the rest of the clan. Yes, only she had eyes that looked as if they'd come from the bottom of a cave. Only her thick, heavy hair matched a moonless night. She had larger breasts than all but nursing women, and although she ate as much as most men, no fat lay under her deeply tanned flesh. Her nose was thin, her mouth full, her cheekbones well-defined.

"Turn around," he said.

Confused, she did as he directed. Because she now faced the wall, she couldn't see what he was doing, but she heard his retreating footsteps on the packed clay floor. Then he returned. "Put your hands behind you."

Again she obeyed. The moment she felt ropes on her wrists, sexual excitement died. Her life from childhood had been about freedom and fighting. As a result of her long training alongside other warriors, she now existed to protect. As one strand became two, pulling her wrists tight against each other, she trembled.

"You hate being confined, do you not?" he said.

"I have never—"

"Never been anyone's prisoner," he finished. "Good. " He turned her around. "Tell me what you are feeling."

Fear. No! She'd never admit that. "The ropes are not so tight that my hands hurt. They are not becoming numb."

"The Kebo warriors bind a prisoner tightly, but I do not think they will do so with you."

There it was. Undeniable words that her role in a future attack on Kebo warriors was to become a captive. Although nothing had changed in the last few heartbeats, she felt even less free, less in control. But she'd never admit it. "You believe they will keep me alive," she said. "But I will go into battle intending to kill the enemy. I will draw blood. They will want their revenge."

He nodded. "That is indeed the way of the Kebo and especially the beast, Haddard, but their women, even those they take as wives, are little more than dumb animals. They grow fat and docile. A beast who believes himself a liege-lord wants to bury his cock in fire."

Before she knew it was going to happen, he again rammed his fingers into her and once more pushed her against the wall. Her roped hands forced her to arch her back, which caused her breasts to act as if they were reaching for him. Her top had slipped down to cover her breasts, but he deftly exposed them again.

She'd seen no more than seven winters when she'd been taken from the old Sakar woman who'd been caring for her and placed in the communal *mogan* with the other future warriors. Perhaps because she'd never felt love for or from the old woman she'd lived with for two winters since she'd been found, she hadn't cried over the separation. Bit by bit she'd come to think of herself as part of a fighting unit and not a separate human being. All warriors relied on and trusted each other. One's strength became another's. One's weakness made everyone vulnerable.

Today she would have no weakness.

"I know many things about the beast, Haddard," Radislay said in a tone she'd never heard before. "His appetite for domination, his cruelty. You will never feel tenderness from him, no kindness. Do you understand?"

His fingers continued working her core, but she refused to let that distract her. "I understand."

"You think you do, but you cannot. Until you are his, you cannot comprehend what brings him pleasure. This." He planted his free hand over her belly. At the same time, he rammed all but his thumb into her and impaled her on him. The twin assaults slammed her into the wall and smashed her imprisoned hands under her own weight. No longer thinking, she fought. She might have wrenched free if he hadn't moved his hand from her belly to her breast and ground his palm against her. He continued to spear her cunt.

"Pain. Fear. Domination. Those things bring him the greatest pleasure," he hissed. "He will demand those things of you until the day you kill him."

* * * * *

Bor, War-liege of the Kebo and next in line behind Liege-lord Haddard, crouched on his haunches. His belly rumbled, his tired eyes ached, and his cougar-claw necklace poked his skin in two places, but he paid little attention to those conditions. As he waited for his lord to speak, he rubbed his thighs, easing his taut muscles. He'd been on his feet since before dawn, first stalking for a lone Sakar gatherer-woman and then grabbing her and bringing her back to where the sometimes nomadic Kebo warriors had set up a summer home. His captive had been so terrified that he'd had to carry her much of the way. Looking at her outstretched and exposed body in the firelight, he wondered why he'd bothered.

Because his liege wanted a Sakar woman.

"She is skinny," Haddard observed as he ran his hands over the captive's prominent ribs. "With no breasts."

"The Sakar keep their women close to the village," Bor pointed out unnecessarily. "This one must be seen as worthless for her to have been out the way she was." No matter how many times he supplied his liege-lord with what the older man loved to bury himself in, he'd never found the perfect captive. Except for the rare female warrior of an enemy tribe, women reminded him more of docile animals than an equal worthy of a Kebo cock. He'd heard of tribes living on the other side of the massive, always snow-cloaked mountains with black-haired women, all of whom craved sex as much as any man, but no Kebo had ever gone there.

And because they hadn't, when a Kebo man needed release, he either spilled his seed in a spirit-beaten slave-whore or serviced a breeder unless there was a fresh captive. In truth, he'd been without a woman for so long that he'd been tempted to take this scrawny creature, but he understood loyalty to his liege.

"Do you want her?" he asked. "Perhaps we should let her go. She knows nothing of warrior plans. I asked."

At his liege's orders, Bor had tied the woman to a tree. He'd chosen one with limbs above her, stretching her arms over her head and wide apart so she could barely move. He'd tugged on the rope until she'd been forced to stand on her toes. Then, because a war-liege's power came from his domination over those lesser than him, he'd cut off her reed dress and placed ropes around her ankles and secured her legs by tying them to small nearby trees. Firelight danced over her outstretched limbs and seemed to settle on her exposed cunt.

"Later. When I am done with her, you can throw her away," Haddard said and got to his feet. "Unless you want her."

His cock did. His cock was seldom satisfied. But the rest of him felt only disgust and disinterest. "No," he said.

"Ah, of course. Only a goddess is good enough for you."

Back when Bor was a youth, he'd thought Haddard the strongest man in the world, but as he'd grown into powerful manhood, Haddard had aged and shrunk. Now Bor stood nearly a head taller than his liege-lord with shoulders wider than any other Kebo warrior and eyes that could see to the horizon. But even as he acknowledged his physical superiority, he continued to respect and obey his liege. Haddard's leadership had made the Kebo the most feared tribe in the vast valley that stretched longer than a man could run in ten days. Other tribes raided and battled. Fighting was the way of life for the numerous tribes prospering in the valley with its rich earth, uncounted growing things, and endless wildlife. But those other tribes feared and ran from the Kebo because Haddard understood their weakness and knew how to exploit it. The Kebo attacked and took what they wanted. They had no weaknesses.

And someday Bor would walk where Haddard now did. And maybe he would find a goddess.

"Does she have life between her legs?" Haddard asked. He stood in front of the whimpering woman but hadn't touched her.

"I touched her there, but she was dry."

"Hmm. And when you grabbed her, did she fight?"

"Only a little and only for a moment."

Haddard gave a disappointed sigh. Looking resigned, he pinched what he could of the flesh over her pelvis. "Why are you so skinny?" he asked in the trade language that made it possible for diverse clans to communicate.

The woman jerked in her bonds. "I do not know. Please, please let me go!"

"What will you do to earn your freedom?" Haddard asked.

"Anything. Suck your cock, master."

At least she knew how to placate her captor, something Bor already knew from listening to her pitiful pleas. After assuring him that she'd always been ordered to go out of earshot when Sakar warriors made their plans, she'd told him about her elderly mother and how her father had been killed by an abuli and how her aunt had been working to have her accepted as a breeder so she wouldn't have to labor as a seed and nut gatherer anymore. Although he'd tied her hands and placed a rope over her neck so he could easily pull her along, she'd tried to rub her body against him. Instead of responding, his cock had remained at rest. Seeing her spread and ready now did nothing for the uninterested organ.

Despite his words, Liege Haddard obviously didn't feel the same way. After pinching and kneading the woman's breasts and doing the same between her legs, he loosened the ropes on her wrists a little. He freed her legs but kept the ropes on her ankles. Then, without so much as glancing around to see who might be watching, he hoisted his loincloth, grabbed the woman's hips and shoved his cock at her. Still whimpering, she arched her pelvis to receive him.

"What about other Sakar?" Haddard asked Bor. He'd buried his cock, but his features revealed nothing of what he was experiencing. "Did you find their village?"

"Yes."

"Good. Good. What about guards?"

"Some."

"And warriors?"

"I did not see many. Perhaps they were out hunting."

"We will soon find out."

As Haddard drove repeatedly into her, the woman jerked and flopped with each thrust. Her expression didn't change.

Feeling nothing himself, Bor rose and walked into the night. She was like countless other women—dumb, unfeeling creatures. A warrior might need the release one of her kind represented, but the moment the warrior was done, he'd forget her.

Why were men alive in every way while women, except for the women-warriors some of the clans had, were more dumb animal than human? Wasn't there a female Kebo with fire? With pride and courage and heart?

A goddess.

Chapter Two

Nuwaa felt as if she was walking in fire. After more battles than she could count on the fingers of both hands, she should be used to the emotions that preceded pitting her skills against those of the enemy, but the anticipation never changed.

Heavily armed, she trotted in the middle of the line of Sakar fighters, her long, single-braided hair bouncing between her shoulder blades, her well-muscled legs effortlessly covering the ground between the Sakar village and where many Kebo warriors had been spotted at a cave at the base of the Blue Mountains. Three days ago a scout had located the Kebo fighters there and watched them long enough to determine that they were readying themselves for a raid but whether against the Sakar or another tribe no one knew. Liege-lord Radislay had assured everyone that the Kebo prepared their weapons and prayed to their spirits for many days before the raid itself, which meant the Sakar could attack before they were attacked.

Although several of her fellow warriors, particularly the two other women fighters, questioned this change in Sakar fighting tradition which called for reaction instead of action, she approved of her liege's plan. Hadn't she watched hawks circle over small, helpless-looking birds, the predator intent on choosing his next meal? But before the hawk could attack, the little birds rose as one against him and chased him off with beaks and claws. Today the

Sakar were many birds. They would peck at the unsuspecting Kebo and kill them. And then, sometime, she'd allow herself to be overtaken but not killed.

The time she'd spent with Liege Radislay continued to run through her mind but didn't distract her from mental preparation for battle. Loving this part of being a warrior, she imagined herself reaching out, out... She floated like a leaf, a butterfly, the wind taking her where it would. She slipped around trees, going deeper and deeper into the forest. *He*, her spirit, waited for her.

As from the first, when an untried girl fasted and prayed alone in the way of countless generations of Sakar warriors, *Wolf* pulled her close. The magnificent hunter and killer stood motionless, yellow eyes glowing from a dark face. When he opened his mouth, she saw teeth capable of silencing life, but her spirit represented no threat to her. Instead, *Wolf* extended his muzzle and touched her outstretched hand in a powerful message. *You believe in me, and I believe in you. I will protect you, and you will place your life in my hands.*

"You are smiling," Tabathi said. "You have been with your spirit?"

Not slowing, Nuwaa nodded at the other woman-warrior. "I feel his strength in my bones and blood."

"I prayed last night," Tabathi said. "It took a long time for my spirit to come to me, and he stayed only a short while."

No warrior ever identified their protector spirit to another human because that relationship was sacred, but that didn't stop Nuwaa from wondering what her friend's experience might mean. "Perhaps your spirit does not understand why the Sakar have become attackers this time."

"Perhaps. I like being predator instead of prey. Our liege has the wisdom of the gods."

"Yes, he does. But…"

"But what?"

"Why is it different only when the Kebo are our enemies?" Nuwaa asked, wishing she felt free to discuss her unique mission. "Always before, we Sakar have defended our village. Our strength is in making sure our *mogans* and the land around it are safe. Let other tribes roam like animals with no place to belong. We become one with the earth beneath our feet, and it befriends and nourishes us."

Tabathi frowned, making Nuwaa wonder if her closest friend hadn't considered that before. "Our liege hates the Kebo leader. I feel Radislay's hatred like an approaching storm."

"So have I. Why is it like that?" Nuwaa mused although she didn't expect an answer.

"It does not matter. The Kebo are like vultures. They believe they can live off the bones of others, that feeding from rotting flesh makes them strong."

Nuwaa laughed. "When I press my knife against a Kebo warrior's throat, I will tell him that. Then I will kill him and leave his flesh to rot."

Tabathi's imagination ran to slicing open her enemy and watching while his guts spilled out. Careful to keep their voices low, the two women expanded on their plans for making the Kebo understand they must never attack a Sakar if they wanted to go on living. It wasn't the first time the two had spoken like this. Words of bravery were as important as prayers to protector spirits in preparing for battle. Slowing a bit to match her pace to Tabathi's shorter legs, Nuwaa concentrated more on the other warrior's tone and expression than what she was saying. Like her, Tabathi had been raised as a fighter. Although she'd been born Sakar, Tabathi had never seemed to mind that her fellow woman-warrior was an outsider. It wasn't the same with the men who, although accepting her fighting skills, never spoke to her of matters outside battle and protecting the tribe and whether she was willing to fuck. Even Ely, the only other Sakar woman-warrior, kept her distance. It didn't matter because a warrior should not think in terms of friendship because a fighter's life might be a short one. It was better to remain a loner focused on staying strong and alive.

But she would die for Tabathi and believed the other woman would do the same.

* * * * *

The sun hung high overhead when the Sakar warriors finally neared the cave where the Kebo had been spotted. At Lorzom's orders, the armed band of fifteen dropped to their bellies and began inching closer. Lorzom, who'd been the Sakar war-liege for as long as Nuwaa had been a warrior, moved at the front of the snaking line. He'd ordered her to position herself directly behind him, something he'd never done before. She assumed he was acting on Liege-lord Radislay's command. In truth, she preferred being here to near the rear because this way she might draw first blood. The hated Kebo would remember her face. At least they would for as long as they lived.

Unbidden, the thought she'd been fighting off all day broke through her defenses. Was Lorzom keeping her near the front because he wanted to be sure the Kebo would see her, try to capture her? And if what made her stomach clench came to be, what then? Could she survive being tied and used until she found a way to cut off the snake's head?

The Kebo had kidnapped one of the Sakar gatherer-women, taken her back to where the entire clan was camped, and kept her for three days and nights. As she told it, she'd been raped repeatedly by none other than Haddard. She'd known it was him because his elaborate and frightening face paint identified him as their leader. Although Nuwaa hadn't had the chance to speak to her, from what she'd heard, the woman had said she wished her rapist had been Haddard's war-liege, a lion-like man whose loincloth had barely concealed his large penis. The war-liege had captured her and easily carried her over his shoulder when her legs gave out. She'd loved the feel of his back on her breasts almost as much as she'd loved listening to him breathing. Yes, she'd been terrified of him, but that hadn't stopped her body from responding.

Gatherer-women were stupid! They did what they did because they looked to be barren and lacked the wisdom to help raise children. If they weren't needed to supply food, Nuwaa would see no use for them. It was far better to be a woman-warrior, to each full moon take the combination of herbs that kept her from getting pregnant.

Sliding along behind Lorzom, Nuwaa thought, not about the coming attack and its possible aftermath for her, but what might happen if she refused to eat the herbs. She couldn't imagine being pregnant, and a woman-warrior didn't speak to a child-bearer about birth, but she'd watched women with babies at their breasts. To hold an innocent life, to whisper words of love, to have value for something other than fighting—

"There," Lorzom whispered.

Well-trained in remaining undetected, Nuwaa didn't try to see what her war-liege was talking about. Instead, she turned to the warrior behind her and whispered, "There." The word quickly traveled down the line. Because Lorzom had laid out his plan earlier, the warriors silently spread out and drew closer to the cave. As she belly-crawled, Nuwaa kept a hand on her sword so not to risk it striking a rock. The grasses here were breast-high and there were enough rocks and brush to cover the ground with a thick layer. But even with *Wolf* beside her, she questioned what they were doing. Over fifty Sakar were warriors. Why had only fifteen been sent on this vital mission? True, the more attackers, the greater the chance of discovery. Still—

Instinct and experience told her when she and her fellow fighters were as close to the cave as they dared get. She'd seen no sign of a Kebo sentry which meant either the enemy believed they were safe here or were stupid. Probably they'd decided to camp in this cave so their wives wouldn't disturb them while they entertained themselves with whatever slave-whores they'd brought with them.

Men were animals! They thought with their cocks.

A sound floated to her and silenced everything in her except preparing for battle. She listened to her heart beating. The solid, steady tones strengthened her. The floating sound had come from the cave, proof that the enemy was in there.

"Now!" Lorzom hissed.

As one, Sakar warriors sprang to their feet and charged. Their yells drowned out their footsteps. A moment later the first Kebo boiled out of the darkness. He was immediately joined by others, all of them armed. Even as she continued to run toward those she'd come here to kill, Nuwaa wondered at the number of men pouring out. There seemed no end to them. The shouts of Sakar and Kebo fighters met. Then the combatants did the same.

Her world barely existed beyond her sword length. As she attacked and defended, her line of sight expanded until she saw nearly everything. Whenever a Kebo entered her space, she either ran her weapon at him or jumped aside. Her legs danced. Her muscles burned. She felt alive. Alive!

The smell of blood filled the air, and she dimly heard a cry that told her someone had been wounded. As long as she stayed on her feet, as long as instinct warned her of danger, her own blood wouldn't flow. Her sword ate into flesh, but she couldn't tell how many times or whether she'd inflicted a fatal blow. The weapon grew heavier so she reached deep into herself for more strength. As always before, her body responded, feeding muscles and bone. In her mind, the Kebo became murderers of Sakar infants. She'd destroy those killers before they could cut down her people's future.

Even as she reminded herself of what had brought her here, the trained observer in her recorded an inescapable truth. The Sakar were overmatched. Fifteen warriors might not be enough to vanquish so many.

No matter! She'd kill as many as she could before she was killed! *Captured?* She couldn't think of that.

Out of the corner of her eye she spotted Tabathi in a standoff with two Kebo warriors. She longed to go to her friend's aid but didn't dare turn her back on the enemy who sought to overwhelm her. Praying Tabathi would be victorious, she turned her attention to the enemy now before her.

This blond-haired man wore a cougar-claw necklace that proclaimed him as war-liege. Perhaps other men matched his size, but she'd never seen any larger. He held himself as a wolf did, proud and sure. Instead of charging her, he stood just beyond her reach. His gaze licked over her. She noted what might be surprise in his expression.

"Fight me!" she yelled. "Wolf against wolf!"

Something that might be either an answering challenge or disbelief flickered over him. He took a step and pointed his sword toward her heart. She'd always wondered what her moment of death would be like and hoped she'd die bravely at the hands of a worthy opponent. This man was worthy, stone-strength and soul-confidence just like her.

"You call yourself a wolf?" he asked.

"I speak the truth. Can you say the same?"

Except for the necklace and loincloth, he was naked. Like her, he'd contained his long hair, although his was tied only at the back of his neck. His large eyes were a rich, deep brown framed by thick dark lashes. His weaponry consisted of a sword only slightly heavier looking than her own and probably made from grizzly bone, but in his hands it became something more. This man, this war-liege, had taken on godlike proportions. Even if she managed to draw first blood, he'd kill her before he died. She believed he had no interest in taking her captive.

Would they die together?

Perhaps.

"A woman-warrior," he said. Yells and other sounds of battle fought to steal his words, but she hung onto them, felt them in her heart. "Come to kill?"

"Yes." Her legs didn't want to move, but she forced herself to step toward him. He extended his sword. *Wolf-spirit, hear me. If you have chosen today for my death, I accept your wisdom. But let me die as a fighter, killing as I am killed.*

Her prayer behind her, she took another step. As she did, movement to the side caught her attention. At the same instant, she heard Tabathi scream.

"No!" she bellowed as crimson gushed from her friend's side.

She couldn't save Tabathi. She could only avenge her. Filled with rage, she charged the large Kebo war-liege. At the same time, she leaned to the side. His sword whistled past, just missing her. For an instant she knew he'd done so deliberately and that he'd also deftly avoided her weapon. Then she crashed into him. His arms closed around her, trapping her limbs by her sides. Screaming, she twisted and turned, kneeing between his legs at the same time. Grunting, he slackened his grip. She thought he was starting to lean forward. Instead, he closed himself around her and held her as securely as if he was a grizzly.

But she was no helpless victim, not with her knife at her waist. Calling on all her strength, she grabbed the hilt.

"No!" he yelled.

"Yes!" she yelled back and stabbed. The knife met resistance. She smelled hot blood.

Then something slammed into the side of her head, and her world flashed red and black. She felt her legs melt, her back turn boneless.

Chapter Three

Hand clamped over his bleeding side, Bor stared down at the woman crumpled on the ground. Pain bit at him. In his mind he repeatedly ran his sword through the creature who'd wounded him, and if she'd been a man, he would have already killed her. Instead, he stared at her long black hair caught in a tight controlled braid that lay over the back of her neck. Most Sakar were pale creatures with colorless hair and eyes that made him think of stagnant water. This creature's eyes were closed, but he remembered staring into midnight. Her skirt had slipped up over her hips as he'd let her drop, and she lay on her belly with her head turned to the side, one leg outstretched, the other deeply bent so he had a clear view of her pussy.

He wanted to grab her there and feel her softness but didn't dare take his attention from the one-sided battle. And he needed to see how badly she'd injured him. After assuring himself that no other Sakar warriors presented immediate danger, he removed his hand from his side and looked down at himself. He couldn't be certain until he'd washed, but old wounds and today's level of pain told him he'd barely be slowed down and was in only minimum danger of developing infection. Still, she'd come close to inflicting a mortal wound.

Angry at both of them, he shoved her with his foot. She looked boneless. No wonder since he'd hit the side of her head with his fist as hard as he could. Unless she was anything but human, she wouldn't soon regain consciousness.

The sense that he was being watched struck him, and he scanned his surroundings. Another woman-warrior lay nearby, her breasts rising and falling as if she'd been running. Then he spotted a Sakar warrior who also wore a necklace that identified him as a war-liege. This man stood apart from the battle, taking in not his fighters, but the unconscious black-haired woman-warrior. For a moment Bor stared back at the other man. Then his enemy yelled something he didn't understand, and as one the Sakar turned and ran away.

"No!" he yelled when his warriors started after them. "Let them go!"

"But—"

"We do not slaughter belly-crawlers. They are not worthy of us."

In truth, his lord would love to shed the blood of every Sakar who had ever lived. As war-liege, his role and responsibility was to follow his leader's orders, but today he had no heart for the task. His life was about pitting himself against his equals in battle, not slaughtering a small band of overmatched foes. Other warriors might take pride from killing the helpless, but he never would.

Although several warriors grumbled about revenge, they contented themselves with loudly recounting their bravery. Two Kebo beside himself had been wounded although none seriously, and were being tended to. Three Sakar lay dead. Most of his warriors' interest was focused on the two female Sakar fighters. A quick assessment of the heavily bleeding Sakar women told him she probably wouldn't live to see the morning, but he ordered her to be carried to a shady spot and a bandage wrapped around her wound.

"You want to fuck her?" an older warrior teased. "If so, you must do so quickly."

"She is yours," he shot back, knowing no Kebo man would rape a dying woman. As he'd directed his men, he'd continued to stand over the strong-looking, black-haired woman. The others had come close so they could study her, but none made a move to touch her. His stance left no doubt that he considered her his.

His? Not once Liege-lord Haddard saw her. And once that happened, she would wish he'd killed her.

Satisfied that his men weren't in any danger, he crouched before the fallen creature. Even before he brushed hair off her cheek, he accepted reality. Yes, the woman was helpless. Yes, he'd vanquished her and would make her his captive in ways she would forever hate, but unless his liege gave permission, no one would bury their cock in her. Haddard was ruler over all Kebo men and the things men did. As such, he rightly laid claim to every prisoner.

He'd want her as his slave-whore and consider her the greatest of prizes.

And he'd expect his war-liege to prepare her for her role by presenting a submissive and sex-hungry female to him.

Holding tight to his emotions, he pulled her legs apart and slid a finger along her slit. She felt moist and warm, alive and inviting. She didn't respond to the touch, but she soon would.

He knew how to turn her into a cunt.

"How does she feel?" the older warrior who'd spoken before asked. "Like every man's fantasy?"

Bor looked up to see a number of warriors standing around, their expressions hungry. He concentrated on not revealing the same emotion himself, succeeding because he'd had seasons upon seasons of burying what his heart felt beneath bravery and dedication.

"Soft," he teased as he sampled her again. "In her prime."

That garnered a collective sigh. Several warriors grabbed their penises and began satisfying themselves. His own ached.

Sudden anger ran through him. He was a fighter, Kebo war-liege! No mere female had ever weakened him or ever would! She was an animal, a prisoner, barely human and certainly not his equal.

She stirred and sighed, the sound faint as a morning breeze. His cock twitched. "Ropes," he ordered. *The time for your training has begun*, he added silently.

Although he sensed he was doing something dangerous, he continued to stroke her labia while he waited for something to bind her with. She tried to close her legs, but her movements were without strength, and he easily kept his fingers where they wanted to be, shifting position so he hid what he was doing from view. The men grumbled. The woman's sigh became a barely audible chant. She started to move her hips.

"You are alive," he muttered. "Ripe." He allowed a fingertip to briefly slip into her opening. "Today you are a flower bud. Before I am done with you, you will blossom and become a great and beautiful flower." He slid in again. "And you will hate me for what I have done to you."

And the lessons will test me in ways you will never know.

He didn't look up to see who had thrown the two pieces of rope at him. Instead, wondering if she was awake enough to know what was happening, he pulled her arms behind her and bound her wrists together. Next, he straightened her legs and tied her ankles, leaving just enough room that she could hobble. He felt resistance from her as he tied the last knot.

A moment later, he rolled her over onto her back and waited. As he did, he touched his side but barely noted the fresh, still trickling blood.

Her black eyes flickered open, closed, opened again. He felt as if he had stepped inside her mind as slow understanding crept over her. After a while, the eyes of slave-whores became like water at night, barely visible. They seemed to have no depth to them as if what they might have or could have become, had died. In contrast, his captive's eyes screamed oaths at him.

"I am Bor," he said, relying on the common trade language that connected all tribes. "I am the Kebo war-liege, and you are my captive."

No, her eyes screamed, but she didn't speak. She didn't move, but he sensed that she was testing her bonds.

"You cannot free yourself because I know what I am doing. Do not try."

Do not tell me what to do, her eyes said. He'd never felt more hated.

Good. You should hate me. "I will not kill you," he said. "At least not now. Maybe I should so I can be done with you, but you intrigue me." Determined to give her a demonstration of what he meant, he dropped to his knees beside her and pushed up her top, exposing her high, full breasts. Her glare intensified. Tradition dictated that he lay claim to her breasts and inflict pain on her so she'd understand, at least a little, the breadth and depth of his mastery. Instead, he regarded the part of her that was woman. A woman's breasts were soft and sensual. They responded to touch and helped bring a woman to the point where she wanted nothing more than to spread her legs. Keeping a slave-whore hungry for fucking took skill, patience, and dedication. He'd long wondered what he could accomplish given time and inclination with a fresh female captive relegated to use as a service beast, but for now little interested him beyond this former fighter's breasts.

On a woman–warrior, breasts were little more than a hindrance and if large enough could get in the way of her ability to fight. Undoubtedly she'd learned how to deal with hers although he was surprised she hadn't bound them. Maybe she understood their ability to taunt and tease and distract a man. *But not me. I refuse to allow you that power.*

"These belong to me," he said and grabbed the hard nipples between thumb and fingers. At his touch, they became larger, even harder, as did his cock. She shifted on the ground but didn't make the mistake of trying to fight him. He'd have to remember her wisdom in such things. "Everything about you belongs to me." Determined to make his point, he squeezed.

She sucked in a breath. Her eyes were like knives.

As he held her, his mind flicked to another scene. Now she stood with her arms wide and tied above her. Her feet too were bound, her stance so wide she could barely stand. He'd shoved a rope in her mouth so she couldn't speak and had placed a rag over her eyes. Despite the gag, she moaned, no longer in hatred but because his cock was inside her. She hung on him, a tethered creature with sweat-slick flesh and cunt muscles trying to swallow him.

He could turn her into a hot and hungry slave-whore with fire throughout her. Even when he freed her, she'd follow after him, touching him wherever he allowed, begging him to fuck her, crying when he left. No other man could make her scream out a climax. No other man would scream from spilling his seed in her.

She'd belong to him and he to her.

In his dreams.

Unnerved because he'd never wanted any woman to have that kind of power over him, he retaliated by squeezing even more. She glared and bared her teeth but gave no other indication that she felt anything. She might still be regaining her senses and too groggy to fully comprehend what was happening, but he doubted it. As a warrior, she knew the importance of constantly assessing her world. Remaining always alert kept a warrior alive.

"Think about this, slave," he taunted. He continued to lay ownership to her breasts but didn't increase his pressure because he wanted her to concentrate on his words. "In the morning, we will start back to where the Kebo are staying. It will take days because we will hunt along the way. I will keep you tied to me, and if I have to leave you to hunt, I will make sure you cannot move. Do you understand? You are mine. Your body, your soul belongs to me. I have become your spirit. If I choose to end your life, you cannot stop me. Your heart beats as long as I want it to."

She still gave no indication of what she was thinking. Angry because he wanted her to beg and make promises that would turn her into a bitch in heat, he pressed against her breasts, flattening them. Their fullness spilled out on either side of his hands.

"I will not rape you." *At least I hope I will not.* "That right belongs to my liege. But by the time I turn you over to him, you will be begging me to fuck you. Whatever you think I might want of you, you will hand it to me."

She started panting.

"Ha, you hear me, slave. Perhaps you do not yet believe me when I say I own you, but you will. You will." Although he should have struck her so she'd remember his promise, he didn't. Instead, he let up on the pressure on her breasts. Her panting became less intense but didn't end.

Despite himself he wondered what it would be like to be under another human being's control, someone who considered him the enemy, and a captor who felt strong and powerful from the act of forcing surrender from him. He felt his own breath quicken.

"Enough!" he ordered, unnerved by the momentary loss of control. Angry, but not knowing where to place his anger, he grabbed her arms and hauled her to her feet. He'd barely given her legs enough freedom so she could stand, which forced her to briefly lean against him. After settling her feet, she straightened and glared up at him. Wanting to see her more clearly, he released her and stepped back. The gesture plainly said he didn't have to hold her to keep her within his control.

Traders who'd come from far beyond the valley spoke of creatures like deer, only much larger, who could be ridden by those who knew how to tame them. At first the creatures the traders called horses fought their riders, but the riders kept them tied and tethered until the horses accepted their new lives. Looking at this woman made him wonder how long it would be before he could ride her. Her eyes said never.

"What do they call you?" he demanded.

She glared as he expected she would. Handing one's name to the enemy was a sign of weakness and surrender.

"I am Bor." He thumped his chest. "Perhaps I will give you a name of my choosing, one which speaks of your captivity."

She tried not to react. He saw the battle in her clenched teeth.

"Yes. You are mine, and I will rename you. But I will take my time. For now you are simply Captive."

Her reaction to the degradation was to straighten as best as she could. Some of the clans of the great and nurturing valley were known for their skill in making the land work for them while others flourished because they were expert hunters. Still others traveled great distances while trading with those they met. He thought of those clans as prey animals because his clan attacked and plundered almost at will. Old men spoke of a time when the Kebo weren't so warlike, but that had been before Haddard came into power. And now that he'd found the Sakar, Haddard had become obsessed with dominating the clan he considered his foremost enemy.

"You intrigue me," he told his Sakar captive. He made as if to touch her again. She sucked in her belly but didn't make the mistake of trying to move. "I have heard of distant clans with your coloring so I know you were not born a Sakar. But you have become a woman-warrior with the clan. I will study you, see what use you might have."

Pulling her to her feet had allowed her fighting clothes to fall back in place, hiding her sex and breasts. Instead of exposing her again, he decided to let her remain clothed so she could think about when and how he'd render her naked. Certainly his decision had nothing to do with the way his body reacted to her.

Someone called his name. He started to turn, which caused his wounded side to protest. He indicated the cut. "I will have my revenge, Captive. You will pay for what you have done to me. Never forget that. You will pay."

Standing straight and strong, Nuwaa struggled to let her enemy's words roll off her. She hated him as she'd never hated another human being. At the same time, she knew hatred weakened a person. A warrior overcome by any emotion risked his or her life. This Kebo who called himself Bor was deliberately taunting her. She had no use for hunters who killed simply because they could. Neither could she consider human someone who was determined to terrify a helpless prisoner.

But even as she accepted the reality of the ropes around her wrists and ankles, the memory of his hands on her breasts, she acknowledged she wasn't terrified. Maybe she should have been, but she didn't believe he intended to kill her, at least not for a long time. This too-big man with muscles better suited for a cougar or bear, spoke of strength she could never equal. Her head still throbbed. Still, she sensed a greater strength in herself. It wouldn't take much for him to strip it from her and reduce her to what he'd threatened — a slave-whore kept so on fire and sex-starved she cared about little else.

"Free me," she taunted. "And I will show you what a real wound feels like."

"A threat?"

"A promise. Are you afraid of me?" She spoke loud enough so hopefully the other Kebo warriors heard. "That is why you have tied me, because you fear me."

"Maybe the time will come when I will let you try to make good on that boast," he said as he clamped his hand over her chin and forced her to look up at him. "But you have lessons to learn first." He stroked her exposed throat. "I feel your life-blood." He demonstrated by pressing against the pulse there. "It would take so little to free that blood. Then what you have caused me to shed would be nothing." He pressed again, threatening to make her lose her precarious balance. "Think on that, Captive. I own your body. I own your life."

Own you. Deep down inside her his words burned and clawed. She'd never loathed another human being as she now loathed him, and yet her emotion wasn't that simple. From the time she'd been chosen for the life of a warrior, she'd learned to assume responsibility for her clan's safety. Her life came after theirs. Her role was to fight and protect, to take risks and perhaps die. She was never without her weapons and constantly trained. She slept and lived with other warriors and only watched the rest of the clan from afar.

But in a matter of moments all that had been stripped away. Completely helpless, she'd become Bor's possession. He held her life in his fingers. Her body indeed belonged to him. And the gatherer-woman he'd caught earlier had been right. This big man's body called out to a woman's. It challenged, promised.

Sudden and unwanted but inescapable hunger slammed into her. Even as she acknowledged the moisture between her legs, she surrendered to fantasy. She had a woman's breasts, hips, and pussy. Men wanted those things. He might have rendered her arms and legs useless, but that didn't give him all the power.

"Be careful of what you say, Bor," she taunted. "Only a fool touches a poisonous snake before he has beheaded it. Even then the fangs are dangerous."

"Ah, but you are not a snake. You are a woman, mine."

Another wave of wet heat flooded her, but at that moment he again released her. She stumbled but managed to keep her balance. As she repositioned herself, she took her first true look at her surroundings. A number of Kebo warriors were staring at her, but what caught and clamped onto her was the body crumbled a short distance away.

"Tabathi!" she cried out. Not thinking, she stepped toward her only true friend. Her ankle bonds stopped and then toppled her.

"Tabathi!" she repeated as Bor caught her.

Chapter Four

Although her captor prevented her from getting any closer to Tabathi, Nuwaa knew the other woman-warrior was dying. Still, she continued to stare at her, not caring about anything else. Tabathi's chest rose and fell, but she'd lost so much blood, her skin was nearly colorless. Blood bubbled around her nostrils. Her eyes were open but filmed as if she'd gone blind.

Only Tabathi had ever heard her dreams and nightmares. Only Tabathi had shared her own fears with her. Sitting together at night they'd sometimes talked about what it would be like to be a breeder and asked why some women were given the gift of creating new life while others, like them, denied themselves motherhood by taking the necessary herbs. At first they'd revealed no weakness. Instead, they'd boasted like the other warriors, insisting that no mere man could kill them before they killed. But bit by bit, word by word, and nightmare by nightmare they'd each learned about the other's heart.

Now Tabathi would no longer fear being wounded, killed, captured. Now she had no one to talk to in her own captivity.

"Go," Nuwaa whispered although she should have kept her emotions private. "Die in peace. Keep me with you just as I will always hold you to me."

She became vaguely aware that she again supported her own weight and no longer needed the loathsome hands that remained on her shoulders. But until she'd helped Tabathi reach the Afterworld, she couldn't think about that. Tabathi breathed slower and slower. A few moments ago she'd moaned softly, but she no longer did. Nuwaa took that as sign that her friend no longer felt pain and thanked Lifelight. Tabathi now had no use for her weapons because in the Afterworld there was no war or fighting.

"Follow your heart," she muttered. "Let it take you to a place of sunlight and laughter, of babies at your breast."

Tabathi took a long, deep breath but not another. Tears flooded Nuwaa, but she fought to keep them inside her. She'd never felt more alone.

"You grieve," the enemy said. He moved so he now stood between her and Tabathi's body. "A true warrior does not feel the emotion."

"Maybe not a Kebo because he is inhuman. It is different for a Sakar."

Certain he would ridicule her further she waited. Instead, he called a long-legged youth over to him. "Run to Liege-lord Haddard and the rest of our clan," he ordered. "Tell them what has happened. Say also that we intend to hunt as we return." He paused, his hands stroking her shoulders. "Tell my liege-lord that I have a gift for him, a Sakar woman-warrior."

He'd called her a warrior, not a prisoner or slave-whore. It might have meant more if she didn't need to finish saying goodbye to Tabathi. Thinking to get close to her one last time, Nuwaa tried to pull free. She didn't care whether she had to crawl on her belly. Maybe the war-liege knew what she intended because he roughly lifted her and threw her over his shoulder. She tried to keep her head up but didn't kick because if he dropped her, she might be injured. The nearby Kebo warriors laughed and said she didn't look like a fighter any more. To her discomfort, she realized that being carried this way had allowed her skirt to ride up exposing her buttocks. Despite her bonds, she tried to reposition the skirt.

"No!" he insisted, effortlessly keeping her in place while at the same time running his free hand between her legs. "Remember, you are mine."

"I will kill you!"

"Not today," he pointed out and walked into the cave. His hand continued to invade her. If only she could kick him!

Darkness closed over her. As she waited for her eyes to adjust to the gloom, he stood her back on her feet. She couldn't tell what he was doing when he walked away, and knew better than to try to move. By the time he returned to her, she'd made out a large, open cavern with a ceiling nearly twice as tall as she was. The cave's walls were covered with jagged rocks, and he'd positioned her so her back nearly touched one of them. Working with the competence of someone who has long handled ropes, he wrapped several lengths under her breasts and around her body. Helpless, she had no choice but to stand there as he then fastened her arms just above her elbows to the rope he'd left dangling behind her. The new tie pulled her arms back but so far it wasn't painful. Next he looped another strand to what was already fastened behind her and tethered her to one of the rocks. She felt cold stone.

"Now you will stay where I want you," he announced unnecessarily. She felt a measure of relief when he removed the ropes from her wrists, and much more sure on her feet as he did the same to her ankles. She managed to take a step but no more, away from the wall. Her hands were free but useless because he'd tied her arms back.

Stepping away, he studied her. "Feel what I have done to you. Think of what I might do next."

With that he seemed to dismiss her. By now the other Kebo warriors had come in. She noted several naked women who'd obviously been in the corners come out. They went about replenishing the fire and preparing meat to be cooked. Looking not at all concerned with the just-completed battle, the warriors settled themselves on animal skin rugs. They occasionally looked at her, but most of their attention was directed at the women who she knew were slave-whores. The men began talking and laughing, but because they weren't using trade language, she understood little of what they were saying. It didn't matter since their animated gestures made it clear that they were recounting their bravery. The more they talked, the more excited they became.

In contrast, Bor sat off to the side, watching silently. He was the only one who didn't look at her. Neither did he seem interested in the slave-whores who kept glancing at the men with expressions that said they knew what was coming and could hardly wait.

The smell of roasting meat filled the air and made her mouth water. She wanted to turn her back on the scene but of course couldn't. Bor hadn't exposed her body. Perhaps she should be grateful because he'd allowed her some modesty, but the rope snugged under her breasts left no doubt of their size or of her erect nipples.

Dismissing their condition, which was beyond her control, she thought of Tabathi. But soon the sense of loss became too great. Maybe, when she had back her freedom, she'd give the other warrior the emotion she deserved.

A woman giggled. Although she didn't want to, Nuwaa turned her attention back to the Kebo. A sitting and cross-legged warrior had pushed his loincloth aside and was roughly directing one of the nude women to sit on his lap. She did so willingly and immediately began grinding herself against him. Although the warrior slapped the woman's breasts trying to get her to take his cock into her, the positioning wasn't right. After a few more slaps, the woman jumped to her feet and stood straddle-legged over him. Her legs were widespread, her knees deeply bent. Hands on her knees, she aimed. As she absorbed him, the man clamped hold of her buttocks and began loudly grunting. A couple of the other warriors watched, as did a slave-whore who was openly satisfying herself. Disgusted with the display and wanting Bor to know what she thought of it, she glared at him. At first he simply sat and stared into the fire, but then, perhaps sensing her gaze, he looked up at her.

"You envy her?" he taunted. "You wish you were fucking instead of watching?"

"They are animals!"

Her outburst resulted in a burst of laugher from several men. The couple engaged in sex paid no one any mind, and now the woman's grunts echoed the man's. Although Nuwaa indeed thought their behavior more animal than human, she couldn't deny that it was easier to watch people fuck than think about her captivity.

Bor's eyes on her reminding her of a hunting cougar, he stood and stalked back over to her. She waited for his hated touch, but he didn't. "These creatures here were once like you," he said. "Free to do what they wanted when they wanted. But that was taken from them just as it will be taken from you."

Maybe she should point out that he'd already stripped her of her freedom but couldn't get the words out.

"Do you want to know how the change is accomplished? How a modest woman becomes a bitch in heat."

"We have slave-whores too."

"Ah. What about it, Captive? Did you help train them? Maybe you prefer being with a woman than a man."

"No!" Between the ropes under her breasts and him standing so close, she had no control over her nipples, which again were turning to stone. She was still damp between her legs and could only hope he couldn't smell her. She'd never thought being bound by the enemy could turn her on.

"Then you need a man's cock?"

This time she knew better than to respond. Armed, she felt the equal to any man. Now, lashed to a wall with her arms dangling helplessly behind her, her weapons had been reduced to her voice and the hatred in her eyes.

She was trying to prepare herself for what he might say or do when the warrior fucking climaxed. He came with a bellow. Although the woman fought for her own climax by continuing to work her cunt muscles against his cock, he threw her from him. She struck the ground and immediately turned back toward him, reaching for his withering cock. This time he kicked her in the belly. Sobbing, she crawled away into the shadows. She'd just begun to masturbate when another warrior hauled her to her feet by her hair and slapped her cheeks over and over again. Nuwaa couldn't understand what he was saying.

"He wants her when he is done eating," Bor explained. "If she has satisfied herself she will be of little use to him."

The Sakar warriors didn't share the same woman in a single day, and most of the time slave-whores were allowed to remain clothed. Most telling, a Sakar slave-whore didn't grovel before a man's penis. For them, sex was what they did, not who they were, at least she thought so.

"There is a difference, isn't there," Bor said as if reading her mind. "Liege Haddard knows a great deal about the Sakar. He says that your slave-whores are as good as dead because they have nothing to live for. It is different for ours because we keep them hot."

How do you do that, she wanted to ask, but of course didn't.

"Think on this, Captive." He slipped her blouse off her shoulder but didn't pull it down enough to reveal her breasts. "I know a great deal about the art of submission. My father trained slave-whores and sometimes I helped him."

She answered him with her eyes.

"You do not believe me?" he asked. "You stand there unable to move and say my skills mean nothing to you?"

They don't. I won't let them.

"A lesson," he said.

Before she could think how she might stop him, he yanked down on her blouse and pulled the rope away from her breasts. They spilled out, prompting several men to stomp the ground in appreciation. Furious, she kicked. Her foot struck his shin. She readied herself for another kick, this one higher and directed between his legs, but before she could deliver it, he'd stepped out of her reach. She strained against her ropes.

"A fighter," he muttered, sounding pleased. "Good."

Staying at a safe distance from her, he walked back and forth, obviously checking to see how much freedom she had and how long her legs were. Despite the uneven battle, she took pride in standing up to him. He might win, but she wouldn't make it easy for him. And she'd die before she became his whore.

"Beat her," someone suggested.

"String her up by her feet," another offered.

The image caused her to shudder, and she turned hoping to see who'd spoken. By the time she'd remembered the war-liege who'd captured her, he'd grabbed another rope and was taunting her with it.

"What are you afraid of?" she demanded, futilely trying to keep him from flicking the rope over her exposed breasts. "You need more ties on an already helpless woman? Such a *warrior*. Call over the others. You must have help."

For an instant she saw a kind of madness in his eyes. He became a fierce animal determined to kill whoever had dared to ridicule him. Then the red heat left him, and he smiled. "This is between you and me, Captive. Until I deliver you to my liege-lord, you will experience my mastery."

"Such power!" she said loud enough for everyone to hear. "You roped an unconscious foe. For that the gods will reward you."

"Silence her!"

"Cut her throat. Let us see her bleed."

"Not before we have all fucked her."

Bor all but growled at his fellow warriors. The slave-whores, perhaps sensing the tension in the war-liege, slunk to the shadows.

"This is between you and me," he muttered. Then, quick as an attacking hawk, he released her from the wall. After looping the rope that had secured her there around his hand, he began hauling her backward deeper into the cave. She tried to resist, but he kept her too off balance for anything, trying not to fall. As he passed a burning brand that had been jammed into a crack in the wall, he grabbed it, lighting their way with it.

They didn't go far, but by the time he stopped, darkness fought only by a single flame, had surrounded her. She felt draped in night, cut off from the sunlight that nourished her. The greater cold in here lifted her breasts. He placed the burning brand in another wall crack. She sensed him closing in on her. Then he lifted her and deposited her facedown on the ground. Instead of stone, she encountered soft fur. Her nostrils told her she'd been placed on an animal pelt. His bed?

Before she could find a way to get off her belly without use of her hands, he straddled her shoulders. She felt his fingers on her, first wrapping a rope around her waist several times, then untying her arms. A heartbeat later, he'd secured one wrist to the waist rope. Although she briefly succeeded in keeping her other hand out of his reach, in the end he won that battle as well. Having her wrists fastened high and against the small of her back robbed her of any chance of leveraging herself off the bed without help, but at least her shoulders weren't being pulled back unnaturally.

He shifted so he now sat lightly on her hips with his back to her and leaned forward toward her legs. She felt his cock brush over her buttocks. Too late she felt a rope circle an ankle. As before, he tied her quickly, expertly, then yanked on her leg, forcing her to bend her knee. When she realized he intended to fasten her leg to the waist rope, she fought like a bird trapped in a net, but he won that battle as well. At least she had the satisfaction of knowing she'd made him sweat.

Facedown on thick fur she had no way of anticipating what he planned to do next. However, instead of completing the hogtie with her other leg, he rolled her over onto her back. He hadn't tied her tethered leg so tightly that her heel pressed against her buttocks but neither could she move it more than a little from side to side. She had to arch her back to keep her weight off her wrists.

Now he stood over her, one leg on either side of her, a hunter admiring his kill. Only she wasn't dead.

"This is how it begins for a slave-whore," he told her as firelight kissed his flesh. If she turned her head slightly she might see his cock, which was barely hidden beneath his loincloth, but she didn't try. Instead, calling on a lifetime of lessons, she watched him. Her helplessness caused her to narrow her thoughts down to one simple reality. She would try to stay alive. And if he decided to kill her, she would welcome death's embrace. A warrior who has died bravely went to a place without battle or weapons, warm land and even warmer sun, endless food and water, willing slaves to meet the warrior's needs, peace.

"What are you thinking, Captive?" he demanded. He held yet another rope, which he'd directed at her exposed pussy.

"Of your blood soaking the ground."

"Not at your hands, Captive." The rope stroked her nether lips. Being manhandled by this war-liege had caused her sex juices to flow. But she wasn't excited, she wasn't!

"I have said this before. I will say it again. For as long as it pleases and entertains me, your body is mine. I can make you hot, turn you into an animal."

"Never!"

"You think not?" Perhaps ready to answer his own question, he positioned himself at the juncture between her legs so her pussy was within easy reach. She couldn't so much as hope to kick with her tethered leg, and he'd forced her to spread her other leg which now pressed against his thigh. "This is mine." He demonstrated by stroking her cunt. "Ah, what is this? The slave is ready for me?"

"Not a slave!" she spluttered. He stroked her again, and although she hated what was happening, some of her anger flowed out of her.

"Not yet but soon." He continued to caress her pussy. In contrast to the way she'd been manhandled up to now, his unexpected and unwanted tenderness confused her. She'd expected to be abused, and she and Tabathi had discussed how they'd handle being raped. She still expected him to force himself on her, but for now she simply lived in the moment.

As the gentle strokes went on and on, she felt herself relax. She should be fighting him. A warrior never admits weakness — never!

But this wasn't weakness. Instead, her thoughts and reactions were being drawn inward. Everything centered around the small hard nub of an organ she'd become an expert at self-stimulating. In the middle of long, lonely nights she'd caress her clit, touch it as no man ever did. She alone had known what she truly needed — gentleness. Something approaching love.

Her captor knew the same thing. How that could possibly be, only brushed against her mind to be lost under soft and flowing sensation. At the same time she felt her heat and wetness grow. The longer he kept after her with life-hard fingertips slickened by her own juices, the more the flowing increased. She no longer felt him just on her clit, her cunt. Somehow he'd found the nerves leading to her belly and pelvis, buttocks and breasts.

Needing more air to breathe, she arched her back and sucked in cool air. It heated before it reached her lungs and added to the fire he'd forced to flame in her. When he leaned forward and blew on her mons, she felt the nerve endings in each dark pubic hair.

No warrior had ever done that to her. Sex between the Sakar was that — sex, bodies fucking during the brief moments not devoted to what it meant to be a warrior. Only she spent time with her body, but never like this. Never!

When he slipped a finger into her opening, she lifted her pelvis toward him. He stroked and glided, causing her to lose the distinction between her flesh and his. In and out he went. Sometimes the strokes were long and deep. At other times, he pumped into her so rapidly she couldn't keep up. She tingled and throbbed, grew hungrier and hungrier. No matter how desperately she tried to keep his finger housed where she needed it to be, her pussy muscles couldn't close down that tight.

If she'd had use of her hands she'd…what? The question faded but quickly resurfaced. She couldn't focus entirely on it, couldn't give herself the answer she'd spent her life preparing. A Sakar warrior fought. A Sakar warrior hated the enemy.

But this enemy was melting her down and turning her into a panting animal that needed more. In a dim way she felt the discomfort in her bound arms, her body's weight on her useless limbs. He'd tied her one leg in such a way that he'd made her completely accessible to him. Her head rocked from side to side in a futile attempt to reduce the growing pressure in her pussy.

She hated feeling like this! She did! She would kill the enemy who'd now run two fingers where they had no reason being and pushed, pushed, pushed into her core.

A moment of sanity returned. Hating her weakness and need as much as she did him, she managed to brace her tethered leg against the ground. Determined to shove him away, she lifted and bent her free leg and planted it on his shoulder. Before she could drive him off her, however, he shifted so her free leg now hung over his shoulder. At the same time, he leaned into her thigh and shoved upward, lifting her lower body off the ground.

Now her weight rested on her upper back and shoulders. During his most recent manipulations, he'd removed his fingers from their temporary home, but as her head thrashed about in helpless denial, he again claimed ownership. By looping his other arm around her raised leg, he managed to bring that hand into play as well. Two and then three fingers now pumped her cave like some endlessly working cock. At the same time, he pressed the heel of his other hand against her mons and began a grinding motion.

"No, no, no!" she chanted. She was probably making so much noise that everyone could hear, but couldn't concentrate on her voice echoing off the walls. "No, no, no!"

A climax bit at her, promising release and speaking of vulnerability. Hating and loving everything about her existence, she tried to wrench away. Her effort at escape caused him to stop his assault on her traitorous woman's body, but only long enough to hoist her ass even higher. He held her in place and supported her with his body. Her free leg bent so that her knee almost touched her face. The other pointed uselessly skyward.

"Feel it, Captive! Feel my power."

Twisting her head to the side, she looked up at him. He leaned over and around her, his strength curled against her weakness. For too long they stared at each other. Firelight both raked his features and softened them. His eyes said things she'd never before seen in another human's eyes. Although she wanted to believe he loathed her existence and took pride in his mastery because that way she could loathe in return, she saw something else. What that something was she couldn't begin to understand or want handed to her.

Then the moment of unspoken communication ended. Powerful fingers gripped her ass. More fingers danced with her nether lips and explored her cunt. His fingers were here, there, everywhere, disjointed and without the rhythm that had brought her so close to climax before. What he was doing no longer paralleled fucking. The fire he'd created in her pussy banked down, but it continued to burn, hot embers that could quickly become a flame again. Now he demonstrated what she took as his disdain of her. Yes, he handled her as an expert hunter handles his weapons, but he wasn't preparing for a hunt. Instead, his treatment said he was simply reassuring himself as to what his weapons were capable of.

Still, the hot embers owned her, and she twisted and turned as best she could. In her mind she saw a speared fish fighting the barbs that had penetrated its belly. The hapless fish still believed it could go on living. It hadn't yet understood or accepted impending death.

"I own you, Captive," he said as he forced her body still higher. "Want me dead, but I still own you."

Chapter Five

Bor rolled his captive onto her belly and untied her arms but kept the leg hobble in place as he repositioned the ropes so her hands were now secured against her belly, held in place by the waist rope. He'd readied himself for a struggle. In truth, he wanted her to fight so he'd be reminded of their relationship. Instead she'd watched him, her expression unreadable. He smelled her sex-awakened body. Although he'd expected his reaction to her scent, he silently cursed his hard cock. As long as he responded to her, he didn't fully control her.

Reminding himself of his task, he hoisted her to her feet and forced her to stand awkwardly on one leg while he placed a rope around her neck and tied it to yet another of the protrusions in the cave wall. Because she wouldn't be able to reach the knot at the base of her throat, he left that rope loose so she could sit or stand as she saw fit. A true master of enemy flesh might force her to stand on tiptoe, but he didn't. As his last act for now, he released her leg. She gingerly lowered her leg, stumbling a bit as she placed her foot on the ground. The hobble had obviously shut off the blood flow.

He imagined she felt even more discomfort in her shoulders, but she kept her pain buried behind her dark eyes.

Dark eyes. Not Sakar-born eyes.

He would have asked her about that, but it was now time for her to be alone in the dark, held in place, smelling her own arousal, asking herself what he intended to do next.

As his final act he positioned her clothes so she was covered again. Then, taking the flaming brand with him, he left.

* * * * *

"You did not make her scream," the thick-legged warrior, Durc, said as Bor began eating. "Cries and moans, yes, but you did not cause pain."

Mindful of Durc's inclination to make a prisoner's existence as miserable as possible, Bor concentrated on the taste of meat charred on the outside but nearly rare in the middle. He hadn't had time to start eating before the Sakar attack and was now ravenous.

"Let me have her for the night," Durc continued. "By morning she will be docile."

"If she is still alive," someone else pointed out. "By the light, Durc, you can be a monster."

"In my hands, the prisoner would get what she deserves." He pointed at Bor's side. "No Sakar belly-crawling insect should shed a Kebo war-liege's blood and live."

Durc was right. The Kebo were feared because of the ruthless way they treated anyone who dared raise a hand against them. Surely most, if not all, of the men sitting around the fire with him were wondering why he hadn't killed her. If he'd attacked out of rage, no one would have spoken against him.

Remembering what she'd looked like lying unconscious on the ground, he amended that. His fellow warriors fully expected him to end her life, but they understood why she was still alive. A body that ripe should be explored first, explored and exploited. That would go on for as long as he wanted, or rather, until he'd presented his prize to Haddard.

Weary of thinking about what the next few days would bring, certainly not because he cared what happened to the captive, he concentrated on his meal. Even as the others boasted of their exploits he didn't add his voice but sat in silence. His side ached dully. It had started bleeding again while he wrestled with her, but no longer.

When his belly was full, he leaned back and tried to concentrate on what the others were saying, but by now he'd heard every boast, every proclamation of bravery. Most of the time he felt at home in this company of men. His strength might come from his own body, but he felt even stronger from feeding off theirs. And he understood how his leadership nourished and sustained them, particularly on nights like this when no one spoke of how little would have had to change for them to taste defeat, for one or more to have been killed.

"You are silent," Durc said. "Your wound is serious?"

"No." Although he briefly clenched his teeth against the discomfort he caused himself, he pressed his side to demonstrate. "It will heal."

Durc laughed. "Then our war-liege's thoughts are on his possession. Go. Take her."

Bor glared at him. "Our liege-lord may want her."

"And you are so faithful to Haddard that you refuse your own body?" Durc teased. "She is the spoils. Just as we took the Sakars' weapons, you can take her." He looked at the others. "No one here will speak of what happens."

Bor knew that was right. Warriors out on their own did what warriors needed and wanted to do. It was the way of men. But when Haddard could no longer lead the Sakar, the role would become his, which set him apart from his companions.

"What happens between the captive and me is for us alone," he said as he got to his feet. "Neither of us will speak of it."

"Certainly not her." Durc's chuckle held no warmth. "Surely the creature trembles waiting for you."

If his captive was indeed shaking in fear, Bor couldn't tell. Although he'd brought a torch with him, he took care not to look at her. He longed to feast his eyes on her lush body, but he knew better than to let himself be distracted…yet.

"There is much I will learn about you," he said, after stretching out on his bearskin bed and resting the back of his head on his hands. He'd been careful to position himself so she could see his strong body and was deliberately careless about placing the loincloth over his cock. Just thinking about her had caused it to spring to life. He could have quieted it by emptying himself in one of the slave-whores, but he preferred the edge sexual hunger gave him. Besides, the whores had long struck him as pathetic animals, and he hated the weakness that occasionally sent him to them. "You and the Sakar."

She didn't speak. In truth, she'd given no indication she was aware of him when he'd returned to her. Interesting. Most of the human spoils of a raid begged and cried for mercy.

"I will tell you what perhaps you already know because I want our thoughts to be on the same thing," he continued. "The Kebo are travelers. When we find a place that nourishes us, we stay a while. But when we have taken what we need from that land, we move on. This valley is rich. Rich beyond anything we have ever seen." His voice trailed off as he contemplated the clean, clear river that ran through rich earth and the uncounted plants nourished by that dirt. "We have already been here for six moons and no one yet speaks of leaving. Truly this place is blessed."

An emotion he'd never felt slid over him, and he wondered what it would be like to spend the rest of his life in one spot, to become one with a single stretch of water, to hunt land that had become as familiar as his own body, to know where he was going to die. To spend his days watching his children growing instead of preparing for battle.

"Soon after our liege-lord brought us here we learned that only one tribe would raise their weapons against us. The others are like deer and run and hide. Our enemies are the Sakar."

She still said nothing, but why should she? He hadn't said anything she didn't already know.

"It is the way of the Kebo to rid ourselves of our enemies, to dispose of them."

She didn't move, and he couldn't hear her breathing. Staring at the ceiling, he half believed she'd somehow gotten free, but he'd seen her small, tethered, yet defiant body when he'd come in.

"The Kebo cut out the heart of the enemy. And the man you call Radislay is the Sakar heart."

This time he heard her sharp intake of breath. "You are surprised I know his name?" he asked. He still forced himself not to look over at her. "I will tell you. Our liege, a man much greater than the belly-crawler you follow and obey, was told this in a spirit dream. Think on that, Captive. Liege Haddard, who is blessed by the spirits and knows everything about the Sakar. When I ask you questions about your warriors and weapons, I already know the answers. But I want to hear the words from your lips. If you tell me the truth, I may let you live. If you lie, I will punish you."

More silence.

"Surely other tribes have spoken of the Kebo. What have you heard?"

He might have been talking to the walls, but although her defiance angered him, he fought for control. Let her contemplate her punishment, let her think of him as a man of stone. With an inner chuckle, he acknowledged that the term fit the state of his cock.

"I may ask you the question again in a few moments, but first I want you to think on this. I have never seen this Radislay, but I know he is not a tall warrior. Yet he has thighs like tree trunks and large feet. His shoulders are worthy of what he wishes to be called. His eyes are weak, his belly so large it slows him. He prefers eating to fighting, but no one has ever called him a coward." He'd been surprised when Liege-lord Haddard told the warriors that because he never praised the enemy. "He is not a cruel man and will not kill if he does not need to, but when he hates, he hates completely. He believes that the only way to deal with those who oppose the Sakar is by putting an end to them. He is an expert with the knife and can throw a spear further than those much taller than him. At least he once could. Has that changed?"

He sensed her eyes boring into him but still refused to acknowledge her presence. Much as he understood his task, he wanted to be learning about her, not talking about the man his liege-lord considered his greatest enemy.

"Are his throws still strong?" he demanded. "Or has age and a soft life weakened him?"

"No!"

"Ah, the captive speaks. You are loyal to your lord?"

"Yes."

"Would you die for him?"

She didn't respond, and her deep breaths didn't supply the answer he'd been looking for. A warrior should gladly sacrifice his or her life for the clan's leader.

"If Radislay ordered you to place yourself between him and the enemy's knives, would you do so?"

"What lies in my heart is not for you to know."

"You are wrong," he bit out and sat up. He thought he'd prepared himself for her shadowy figure, but her defiance in the face of her captivity struck him like a blow to the belly. He'd left her without the freedom to take more than a few steps, and she had no use of her hands. Still, her glare was as powerful as his own. *Kill me*, it said. *You can end my life but you can never destroy my heart, my courage.*

For several unguarded moments he hoped he'd never have to. She was life, self-pride, defiance, a warrior through and through. If he'd been the one in ropes, his reaction would be the same. He might be physically helpless but nothing would ever touch his heart. He'd die without knowing the taste of fear.

Or at least without acknowledging it.

Hating the unwanted thought, he stood and walked over to her. She followed his every muscle move, didn't try to back away. Not sure what he had in mind, he reached out and took hold of her long dark braid. It felt like flowing water. The cool strands began heating in his grip, and he moved his fingers closer to her scalp. Tense and barely breathing, she stood as stone. A Kebo warrior's mate was chosen for him by the clan's elders. Once mated, a warrior's sexual needs were satisfied, certain fires kept tamped down, but until that happened, release came only from the slave-whores. Haddard had told him that although he'd spent a great deal of time thinking about this, he'd found no Kebo free woman worthy of the clan's war leader. If Bor so wished, he could select one of the slave-whores as his own until Haddard's youngest daughter was old enough to mate.

Tonight he wanted to mate with this nameless captive, but she didn't. She'd never want that.

Torn between needs of the flesh and the weakness he knew he'd feel if he took his captive, he continued to stroke her hair. He imagined her letting it down for him, the rich strands flowing over her neck and shoulders, losing his fingers in the thick length.

"Do you have a mate?" he asked.

For several heartbeats she said nothing. Then, "No."

"Why not? You are of age."

"I am a woman-warrior."

"I am a man-warrior. That would not stop having a mate chosen for me."

"It is different for a Sakar woman-warrior." She still hadn't moved but didn't seem quite as tense. "When a woman mates she, she…"

"What?"

"Wants to become a mother."

And your liege-lord sees more value in you as a warrior. "What about fucking?"

"What do you care?"

He increased his grip on her hair and pulled her head toward him until it rested on his chest. "I want to know, Captive. When a Sakar woman-warrior needs to fuck, what does she do?"

"She tells another warrior and he services her."

He all too easily imagined two sex-hungry bodies coming together because that's what it was like for him. He'd studied Liege-lord Haddard's young daughter trying to imagine the girl as his mate, but although he could see the still-dormant woman's body beneath the straight lines of her body, the girl laughed and played and only reluctantly helped her mother cook and create clothes. He couldn't imagine her caring about a mate's needs, a mate's thoughts and heart.

"Is there a Sakar warrior you want as your mate?" he heard himself ask. He continued to hold her so her head pressed against his flesh. She felt smaller now than she had before, less an enemy. He should have pulled off her clothes so she'd understand even more how much command he had. Belatedly he realized she hadn't answered. "Who do you want as your mate? Was he with you today? Perhaps he ran, leaving you to your fate."

"There is no one." Her voice sounded muffled.

No one. Like me. "Why?" he asked and released her. She straightened, then changed position so she faced him again.

"I do not know," she whispered after another of the silences he was becoming accustomed to. "I watch our warriors. I see them at rest, preparing for battle, fighting. But none touch me."

He wasn't sure what she meant, or maybe he didn't want to acknowledge that what she'd said echoed his own thoughts. Before he could decide whether he wanted to hear her voice again, one of his fellow warriors began a rhythmic grunt, grunt, grunt. He'd heard the sound enough times to know Durc was fucking a slave-whore. By the way his captive cocked her head in that direction, he knew she too understood what was happening. Much as he hated Durc's fuck-cries, he imagined himself doing the same thing. If he buried his cock in a soft, wet pussy, he'd sleep as the dead tonight. And in the morning, he'd look at his captive as a hostage of war and not a woman. Maybe.

A slight movement on her part pulled his thoughts off Durc. For a moment he thought he'd imagined it, but then she shuffled her feet again. She no longer held her head as high and her shoulders had sagged slightly. This proof of her exhaustion struck an identical chord in himself. Although he would never admit it to another human being, fighting to stay alive took its toll on him. Besides, he'd lost blood today.

"I am ready to sleep," he said. "And you will be beside me so you cannot escape."

Chapter Six

Her captor used the rope around her neck to lead Nuwaa past the Kebo warriors and outside. Although she hadn't wanted to acknowledge the enemy, her attention was drawn to the loud sounds of fucking in a corner. She saw a naked woman on her hands and knees with her ass exposed. The man riding her stood behind her, gripping her buttocks as he drove his cock repeatedly into her anus. With each thrust, the woman's body rocked forward, and she looked in danger of falling onto her face. Nuwaa couldn't be sure because of all the noise the man was making, but she thought the woman was silent and imagined her counting the moments until the assault was over. From what she could tell, the man wasn't yet nearing climax. The others paid them no mind. Instead, their attention shifted from whatever they'd been talking about to her.

"Leave her out in the cold," one man suggested. "By morning she will be docile."

"You think our war-liege wants her anywhere but with him," another countered. "Bor, if you tire of her, I will take what is left."

That prompted several others to offer their thoughts on what they'd do with her, but Bor didn't slow his pace, and in a moment they were outside, away from the hated voices.

He continued to pull her after him. The moon tonight was thin and weak, and she had to concentrate on each step. She hated everything about what was happening to her, perhaps nothing more than not having use of her hands. For a warrior, her body was as much a weapon as her knives, swords, and spears, but he'd secured them against her belly with the waist rope. She tried not to think about the humiliating rope around her neck, but it rubbed against her flesh, making that impossible. She felt like a captured animal.

Bor stopped abruptly, turned from her, and urinated. His grip on her tether didn't slacken and even if she'd managed to jerk free, where would she run in the dark? He knew this land much better than she did. And he had use of his hands.

"Go." He jerked down on the neck rope.

Pressure on her swollen bladder had been making it hard for her to concentrate on anything else. Although she'd always performed this act in private, she waited only a moment before doing as he commanded. By spreading her legs as wide as she could before squatting, she managed to keep her skirt out of the way. The smell of her urine mixed with his, reminding her of certain basics they shared. She clenched her muscles several times to dry her opening, then stepped away from what of herself she'd spilled onto the ground.

Instead of taking her back inside, he stared up at the sky. She heard him mutter something under his breath and guessed he was praying to his spirit. Closing her eyes, she did the same. In her mind she saw the great fog-gray wolf who'd come to her when she'd gone on her spirit search. She first spotted it standing in the night, then coming closer and closer until she felt the heat caused by its breath. Its presence strengthened her and threatened to bring tears to her eyes.

Be with me in my time of captivity, she prayed. *Keep me strong and let me complete my mission. When I have buried a knife in the heart of the Kebo liege-lord, I will place my body, my life in your care. If I am to die then, I accept. But, please, do not rush my end because first I must accomplish what my liege-lord ordered.*

She should stop. She had nothing else she wanted or dared ask of her spirit. Still, she couldn't silence her thoughts.

I have been taken by a man unlike any I have ever seen. His strength is great. He says things that touch parts of me I did not believe possible. I fear he will continue to touch me and to seek to change me and make me weak. I walk only when he says I should. Sleep only when he allows. He touched my breasts and sex, but instead of loathing him, I wanted it. I felt heated. Different. Please, keep me strong. Do not let his hands or words weaken me.

With a start, she realized Bor was looking down at her. There was so little light that she barely made out his form, but she had no doubt his attention was on her. "You have a spirit?" he asked.

"Yes."

"And you were praying to him?"

She straightened. "Yes."

"Asking him to help you kill me?"

She should have been, shouldn't she? Night slid around her, around both of them. For as long as they remained outside, it was as if they were the only two humans in the world. She could speak to no one else and sensed no other presence. This man already knew so much about her. He'd plundered her body and learned many of its secrets, and as long as he lived, neither of them would ever forget that. Maybe he even sensed what was in her heart better than she did. The thought caused her heart to hammer.

"It does not matter," he said, "because I will not allow that to happen." With that, he started back toward the cave, taking her, his possession, with him.

The fucking man had finished and was standing where she and Bor would have to pass close to him. "I knew it," he said loudly. "Others said you would leave her to shiver in the dark, but she has more value with her legs spread and ready for you."

She hoped Bor wouldn't stop. Instead, he did so, so abruptly she nearly ran into him. The neck rope transmitted her captor's increased grip. "What I do to her is not for your eyes and ears, Durc. I answer to only one man — Liege-lord Haddard."

"You are too serious." Durc made as if to punch Bor on the shoulder but stopped just shy of the contact. "I envy you your prize, that is all." Durc's fingers snaked out. He captured a nipple through her top and gripped it so hard she was forced to breathe through her nostrils. "Ripe," Durc announced. "Full. Not an old woman's breasts." Despite his teasing tone, he kept his attention trained on Bor. "You are blessed, War-liege."

When he abruptly released her, it took all her restraint not to land a foot blow on his cock. If she hadn't believed his retaliation would be swift and brutal, she would have. Raging at Durc when her anger should have remained locked on Bor, she belatedly realized that Bor had merely grunted before dragging her back into the cave's recesses.

Once they'd returned to where he'd kept her before, he turned her away from him and slid the neck rope so the knot was at her back. Then he circled another rope under her breasts and tied that one behind her. Next he ran another cord between the two ties, securing each knot where she couldn't reach them. Only then did he release her still tied hands from her waist and secured the neck tether to his much larger wrist.

"We sleep," he said, dropping to his knees on the bearskin ground cover.

She remained standing as he stretched out on his back, but when he jerked on the rope, she had no choice but to join him. The bedding under her knees felt soft and luxurious and more appealing than the woven reed blankets the Sakar used. Even as she tried to prepare herself for sleeping beside him, she surrendered to the appeal of being surrounded by softness. True, her stomach growled, but now that she'd given herself permission to sense her body's needs and messages, she realized she was exhausted. After a brief hesitation, she positioned herself on her side, facing away from him. She waited for a harsh invasion of flesh. Instead, he simply sighed twice and began the slow breaths that said he was asleep.

At first the sounds grated on her overloaded nerves, but before long she began to relax. She hated that he'd already learned so much about her body while she had little knowledge of him, but hadn't her own people done the same with captives? Isolating a prisoner from what was safe and familiar while forcing him or her to endure whatever the Sakar captor saw fit to subject the prisoner to had proven to break that prisoner down in ways beatings couldn't.

She'd have to remember that everything Bor did to her might be calculated to break her will. He could force her to answer his questions, then suddenly turn silent or rob her of her voice and sight. Hadn't she done the same herself once with a trader who'd foolishly believed he could steal Sakar weapons? By the time she'd released the unfortunate man after two days of leading him around blindfolded, he couldn't run fast enough. No one had known she'd discovered him while she was guarding a hunting party because she'd kept him tied and gagged a distance from the village. As for why she'd decided to fill the trader with dread instead of killing him...

Shivering slightly, she realized she'd briefly fallen asleep. She might have wakened because her awareness of her situation had been impossible to ignore but more likely her cold back was responsible. For several moments she fought the urge, but the need for sleep nibbled at her. Wondering how he'd react, she scooted toward her captor until she felt his body heat. The warmth reminded her of his greater size, but if he insisted on making her sleep with him, why shouldn't she take what he had to offer?

No longer cold, she tried to put her mind on what opportunities for escape might present themselves over the next few days, but no matter how much she relished the idea of outrunning War-liege Bor, she couldn't forget why she was here — to kill the Kebo leader.

How? I have no weapons. Have you sent me on an impossible mission, one I will surely fail at, one destined to end with my death?

And what would Bor demand of and from her before she died? The thought of what he might be capable of should have filled her with loathing and hatred. Instead, she felt wet heat between her legs and had to fight the urge to turn toward him and lay her body over his.

Giving in to what belonged to her and the night, she imagined him awakening and lifting her up and onto his body. Eyes closed, she'd spread her legs on either side of his hips and position her so her woman's place was over his hard, dark cock. Smiling a little in anticipation, she'd draw out the moment when she'd take him into her. He'd grip her thighs, his breath coming fast, lifting his pelvis. She'd open her eyes and look down at him, feeling her power and their shared need. Her sex-smell would fill the small space, and the walls would shelter them from the world.

Slow, so slow her legs threatened to cramp, she'd lower herself onto and over and around him. Despite his cock's great size, he'd slide easily into her. She'd fill herself with him and feed off his soft-hard offering. By now she'd be on her knees, leaning forward and bracing herself on his chest. They'd be so close that his features blurred, but she'd know he was acknowledging her power. A man was weak, muscles and bone and weapons reduced to nothing when presented with a woman's body. At those times he was ruled, not by his clan's need for him, but by the demands of his cock. She'd command him with her cunt, enslave his cock, make him beg for release.

She'd laugh at him, tensing and relaxing her muscles by turn while threatening to leave him before he could come. Desperate and determined to keep her with him, he'd go from pressing his fingers into her thighs to stroking them. He'd stop trying to drive his cock through her and gentle his strokes. He might call her handsome, might say he loved the weight and texture of her breasts. He might even speak of gifting her with his seed, giving her his child.

Tears burned behind her closed lids. Even as she slid her bound hands between her legs to caress hungry, weeping flesh, words no man would ever speak echoed inside her.

* * * * *

Running. Laughing. Feeling the wind in her hair. Hearing other laughter and turning to acknowledge the girl running beside her.

Oblivious to anything except the race, she set her mind to outstripping Tabathi. They were no longer women-warriors but the girls they'd been when their friendship had been born. By unspoken agreement they'd slipped away from the hunting lesson and gone in search of berries. They'd found large, sweet clazberries on a sunny hillside and shoved them into their mouths as fast as they could. One of them had asked what they'd do if a bear or abuli decided to come there to feed. Suddenly nervous, they'd agreed they needed to return to the others. Perhaps Tabathi had been the first to start running. Perhaps she'd initially given in to the impulse.

Whatever the seeds of their impromptu race, they now ran side by side. Sweat dripped off young flesh. Still-growing breasts jiggled. Naked and shoeless, they raced, fed by youth and endless energy. One might briefly outstrip the other. Then the laggard would pull even more determination from deep inside and draw ahead. They ran without regard to saving any energy for later. They ran because they could, because they shared the same love of life, of freedom.

Tabathi was her friend, the one person she entrusted with her flickering memories of life before she'd come to live with the Sakar. In turn, she listened intently as Tabathi told her of the fights between her parents and her vow to never let a man hit her as her father hit her mother. They said nothing about keeping this pact of silence. It wasn't necessary.

* * * * *

A deep rumbling voice seeped into Nuwaa's consciousness. At the same time she felt herself being pulled around so she was now surrounded by a larger, stronger body. She came awake as a warrior is taught, swift yet silent. Without needing to open her eyes or allowing her muscles to tense, she knew Bor had turned her toward him and had wrapped his arms around her. She felt his heart beating against her breasts, his leg looped over hers. His erect cock scraped against her flesh.

"You are crying," he whispered. His voice carried remnants of sleep.

"No. Never."

"Yes." He proved his point by briefly releasing her and running a forefinger over her lashes. Even before he deposited the hot moisture on her cheekbone, she knew he was right.

I do not cry. Not ever.

"Were you asleep?" He still whispered.

"Yes," she admitted because he'd made her part of him.

"A dream?"

"Yes."

"What was it?"

The dream had returned even before he'd asked. In her mind and heart and soul she *saw* Tabathi lying on the ground. So much blood had soaked the earth that surely it had all drained from her, and yet the killing wounds continued to bubble and run red. Tabathi's open eyes had filmed over. Her heart no longer beat. In the dream, Nuwaa had knelt beside her and chanted the prayers that would send her friend into the afterworld. Then she'd dipped her fingers in Tabathi's blood and smeared it between her breasts. She'd been trying to gather the strength to stand when Bor's touch had shattered the necessary leave-taking.

"Nothing," she started to say, but Bor's heartbeat became stronger, and her woman's place now heard the sound. "I was saying goodbye."

"To the dead woman-warrior?"

"Yes."

"And shedding tears for her?"

"She was part of me."

Although she expected Bor to demand a further explanation, he remained silent as he began stroking her back. The torch had gone out. The enemy warrior existed only in the kiss of flesh to flesh, of words spoken in the darkness, in whatever residue of tears his fingers still held. Instead of trying to separate herself from him, she snuggled into him and lost herself in an embrace that existed only in her memories. Once, perhaps, her mother had tenderly stroked her. The ancient touch, maybe, had taught her the meaning of safety, of belonging, of being loved.

Her captor didn't love her. He never would. But in this time and place the world couldn't reach, they'd ceased to be who they were. They'd become—what? Man and woman?

"I understand," he muttered. "I had a brother, born on the day of my birth." He'd been caressing her shoulders, but now his fingers started moving down her spine. "When I looked at him, I saw me. Only our mother could tell us apart. We grew up side by side, speaking with the same voice, our muscles and height and thoughts the same."

He fell silent. More tears dampened her lashes.

"He was killed the first time we went out as warriors."

I am so sorry. "And you felt as if you had lost a part of yourself," she managed. She couldn't say how she knew this, just that she'd somehow slipped into the mind of the youth he'd once been.

"I have never found that part again," he whispered. "It slipped into a bottomless hole and no longer exists."

"Did it or have you denied it?"

His searching fingers stilled, but he made no move to shove her away. "I do not know," he said after a brief silence. "I have never asked myself that question."

"Just as I do not try to remember my mother."

"Your memory of her has fallen into the same hole where my brother rests."

It seemed impossible that two people separated by clan hatred could have anything in common, but weren't their bodies searching for connection? Overwhelmed by the question, she shifted position so she could reach for him. Her fingers found his chest, and she flattened them against his heat.

A humming sensation sprang to life in her woman's place, and although she shouldn't, she let her focus shift to there. She understood the need to fuck. Sometimes at the end of a battle, the need to tap into the part of her not devoted to protecting the clan rushed over her like a violent storm. When that happened, she went in search of a cock to fill her. The men must feel the same way because they'd always sensed her need and presented themselves to her. Once another Sakar warrior had grabbed her and thrown her to the ground, pinning her down with his heavier body. Instead of fighting him, she'd spread her legs and welcomed him in.

The same need now stroked her flesh and heated her blood. Ignoring her tethered hands, she caressed her captor as he'd done her. As she stroked and pressed, feathered and tested, she felt his belly tighten. She hadn't yet touched his cock, but because it probed at her, she knew he was fully erect. He'd gone back to exploring her spine, sometimes pressing against the small of her back so it felt as if his fingertips had reached clear through her. She imagined his fingers, not on her spine, but in her. His life-hardened hands would explore what belonged to her, not because she belonged to him, but because she wanted what he offered and he knew her desires. She'd open herself to him, offer him the part of her he wanted most. At the same time, she'd accept the gift of his body, his cock.

His cock.

Not asking herself what, if anything, she had in mind, she scooted lower and slipped her fingers around his man-organ. He tensed but didn't pull her off him. In her mind she saw swollen veins and rigid, reddened flesh. Her fingertips found the fine hairs around his balls and the loose skin that protected his penis. Breathing raggedly, he folded himself around her, grabbed her buttocks, and pressed her against him. For a moment she accepted the increased confinement, but he'd given her access to what made him a man. She needed, wanted to acknowledge the gift in the only way that mattered.

Although he might misinterpret her intentions, she pushed on his shoulder to let him know she wanted him on his back. Although he propped himself up on his elbows, he did so. Grateful for the night, she spread his legs and positioned herself between them. On hands and knees, she lowered her head, searching until she found him. She touched her tongue to the tip and tasted the single wet gift. He fell back and arched his spine, reaching out until he found her rope-circled breasts. He cupped them and squeezed their hanging weight, his grip letting her know he'd punish her if she tried to harm him.

Understanding that neither of them trusted the other, she nevertheless lapped at him. Her ass stuck up in the cold night air. She felt her own wetness. Again and again she ran her tongue around his tip but couldn't say why. Maybe she needed to demonstrate her small measure of control. Maybe she needed to taste what was male about him. And perhaps being a captive had made her insane.

Whichever it was, she went from simply dampening him with her tongue to sucking first his tip and then a little of his length into her mouth. Because she had limited use of her hands, she rested her upper weight on her elbows and pressed the heels of her hands against the base of his cock. The ropes on her body no longer repulsed her. Instead, they became part of the impossible connection between them.

Her world closed down. It existed no further than his cock, her exploration of it, his fingers gripping her breasts, her lonely and hot pussy. She imagined his cock filling her, absorbing her, but this was safer. Maybe.

She didn't know she was going to do it until she opened her mouth wider and touched her teeth to him. He grunted and closed his fingers around her nipples. They held each other, testing their separate control. Then because she knew she would not hurt him tonight, she opened her mouth even more and used her tongue to stroke where her teeth had been. For his part, he began rolling her nipples between fingers and thumbs, caressing her again.

She'd never held a man like this before and only half comprehended what she was doing now. If he demanded to know why she'd have no answer.

In her mind it became morning. The sun had found this inner corridor and was providing enough daylight that she could see his expression. No longer did his eyes say she was the enemy. Instead he acknowledged that she was a woman, alive and hungry. She'd turn her famished gaze on him. He'd smile the smile of a man who understands women before impaling her on him. She'd hang there, lost with him inside her, breathing hard and fast, growing hotter and hotter, feeling some force growing and becoming powerful. The power centered around her clit but reached everywhere.

She dimly realized that he'd released her breasts but gave no thought to what he intended to do until he grabbed the neck rope and pulled down on it. Alarmed, she released his cock. The next moment she found herself held tight against him with her face smashed into his belly. Her hands were trapped under her, giving her no way of pushing herself off him.

He shifted his grip to the back of her head but instead of punishing her, he ran his fingers into her hair and along her scalp. Because her nose was against him, she had to fight for what bits of air she could get into her lungs, but she didn't fight. Something about their position, his cock held tight between them, again spoke to that part of her she'd never known existed.

After a lifetime of seeking control over her world, she welcomed the opposite. He could kill her. She'd understand why if he sliced open her throat. But she lived in the moment, feeling his strength and acknowledging her weakness. She'd taste his flesh and pray he wanted to do the same.

"Up," he abruptly ordered and shoved her up and onto her knees. She knelt between his splayed legs, waiting.

Chapter Seven

She didn't move as Bor sat up. When he untied the ropes around her neck and breasts, she'd concentrated on trying to keep her breathing regular. Although she hoped he'd free her hands as well, he didn't. Still, his efforts told her that something had changed between them. Their roles were no longer cleanly defined as captor and captive.

But what had they become?

"Lie down," he ordered. "On your back."

Trembling, she did so, placing her hands over her navel. The humming at her core demanded too much attention to allow her to close her legs completely.

After sliding to her side, he grabbed her bonds and positioned her arms over her head. She could have brought them down again but didn't, and when he pushed her skirt up around her waist, she lifted her buttocks off the bearskin.

"A warrior must not allow his possession to take control of his man-organ," he said, his voice thick. "It will not happen again, understand."

"Yes," she said even though that was the last thing she wanted. She'd loved the feel of him in her mouth, not the power but because she'd needed the gift.

"You are mine, not the opposite." He demonstrated by running his hands along the insides of her thighs and spreading her legs. Again she struggled with her love-hate reaction to the night. "This belongs to me." He touched her nether lips. "And this." He dipped into her to gather some of the seemingly endless moisture. Unable to breathe, she ground her buttocks against the fur. If only she dared wrap her arms around him!

"Whatever I want of you I will take," he told her. He closed his fingers around her hot labia and pressed them together. "Understand."

Words of submission. Words of control.

"Do you understand?" he repeated. He punctuated his question by pulling on the loose, hot flesh.

Caught between pleasure and pain, she writhed under him. To be held like this by a man, by the enemy —

"This is mine," he muttered.

He still drew on her lips but also slid the separate folds against each other. Her juices eased the journey, and the hot sensation increased, causing her to roll her head from side to side. She could no longer feel her legs.

"I wish to drink from my prize," he whispered. "You will feed my thirst."

For a moment she had no idea what he was talking about. Then he released her and blew his moist breath over what he'd just claimed, and she whimpered. She thought he might have chuckled. After lubricating what needed no more moisture with another breath, he forced her legs even further apart. She danced to his touch.

"Be still," he warned.

She tried, but her body's needs made submission impossible. Moaning, she lifted her pelvis toward him. He pressed a hand against her belly. His other hand went under her buttocks. His mouth closed over her cunt.

Remembering how she'd used her teeth on his cock, she stopped moving. If he started to punish her, she'd fight, but he was so strong. Even if she managed to hold him off, his fellow warriors could easily immobilize her.

Thoughts of the punishment he was capable of inflicting briefly distracted her from what he was doing. By the time she'd caught up to him it was too late because he'd bent a leg so her foot rested against the inner thigh of the other. The new position kept her apart and ready for him.

Now—

By all that was sacred, he slid his tongue into her weeping opening! Sobbing, she arched her back as best as she could off the fur. Her arms became too heavy to lift. Again, again, again he lapped. With each stroke, her belly clenched and her pussy muscles trembled.

She spread her legs for a Sakar warrior because she craved the sensations that accompanied clenching, shaking muscles. Always before, release had come with a cock in her or when she'd worked herself to climax, but now her captor owned her with nothing more than his tongue.

She moaned for him. Moaned and sobbed, and over and over again fought to increase his access to her. His tongue flamed her here, there, everywhere, taunting and torturing. Somehow he knew when she hovered on the brink of release and shifted his torture elsewhere so she continued to hang.

"Please, please, please," she heard herself chant. Once again her body was on the move. She couldn't control the direction or pace of her hot muscles and couldn't think beyond the kiss of wet flesh against wet flesh. She wanted to close herself off from him. She wanted to remain like this forever.

"Let me—please, let me—"

With a grunt, he shifted between her legs and raised the bent one so it now lay over his shoulder. He slid his hands under her buttocks and lifted.

Then his tongue returned, and she cared about nothing else. Because of the adjustments he'd made, he was able to drive his tongue even deeper into her. But although she felt as if she might pass out, the promising climax continued to remain just out of reach. If only he'd touch the nub she'd learned to manipulate to release! If only he'd end this sweet punishment!

"Please, please, please!" Her head thrashed. She thought of grabbing his hair and yanking him away, but her arms remained where he'd placed them. "Oh please."

Flashes of light filled her vision, and she cried out. He made a sound like laughter and continued to probe and lave.

She had no idea how long she'd been like this with her muscles so taut everything trembled when he slid his hands out from under her buttocks and abruptly sat up. The sudden loss of sensation at her core forced a sob out of her. Although she knew it would no good, she tried to look at him.

"A lesson, Captive," he spoke roughly. "I allowed you to demonstrate your mouth's skill with my cock. Now you know of my mastery."

She felt like a puddle of water. Not a single muscle remained. She couldn't stop the silent, hungry tears.

"Do you understand?" he asked. "The power is mine."

Yes.

The thought made her clench her teeth. This man, this enemy, had turned her into a whimpering animal, and she wanted to hate him for it. But hatred wouldn't turn his words into lies.

"What is it, Captive?" He roughly pressed her legs together. "I have left you hungry?"

"Yes," she admitted because the word escaped before she could stop it.

She thought he'd throw her admission back at her. Instead, he continued to kneel over her. After squeezing her thighs again, he ran his hands up and over her pelvis. Sweat dripped from the small of her back to be absorbed by the fur. Despite the clawing hunger still nestled between her legs, she started to think. He might be reinforcing his superiority, but the hard, hot length she'd recently held in her mouth had told her something about him. She wasn't the only one who needed release.

By concentrating, she managed to lift her arms up and down. Instead of resting her hands on her belly however, she grabbed his cock. As she suspected, he hadn't lost anything of his erection. He could have struck her and forced her to release him, but he didn't. Instead, he continued to press down on her pelvis. They held each other like that for a moment while she struggled with equal amounts of power and helplessness.

"Hunger has two faces," she whispered as she rolled his cock between her cupped hands. "One for the woman, the other for the man."

"But only one way of feeding the hunger," he said.

Before she could guess what he had in mind, he grabbed a calf and again bent her knee. He used his hold to press her leg up and against her belly. His manipulations had caused her to release his cock, and she didn't know what to do with her hands. As he'd done before, he settled himself between her legs and lifted her.

Understanding, she scooted toward him and offered herself to him. The first time he drove himself at her, his cock struck flesh. He expertly repositioned himself and slid in, filling her, making her part of him. She placed her hands over his head so the rope between her wrists rested against the back of his neck. The sweat he'd caused to break out on her earlier returned in force, and she took him deeper, deeper.

She felt his breath on her face but sensed he had no desire to touch his mouth to hers. Good. She might give him her woman-place. She'd never give him tenderness.

They fucked, animal need meeting animal need. He'd brought her so close a few moments before that blood had already pooled in her core. His great and insistent organ opened her, and she rode with him, thrust meeting thrust, sobbing out ragged breaths. His flesh became hers. Hers flowed into his.

And she came.

Came again.

The third time her muscles spasmed, she screamed and briefly lost consciousness.

* * * * *

A faint flickering red light reached where he'd spent the night with his captive, but as Bor woke, he gave little thought to the morning fire. His captive lay on her side turned away from him, but he'd placed his arm over her in his sleep, and she remained under his control. With consciousness came more memories. He'd removed every rope except the one on her wrists. More, much more, he'd turned his penis over to her and let her rake her teeth over what meant so much to him. Yes, he'd demonstrated his domination by tonguing her, which was something he'd never done to a woman before, but only after she'd left her mark on him.

Then they'd fucked.

Fuck?

A captive could be raped at will. No one would have tried to stop him if he'd decided to ravage her and she'd probably expected to be taken violently. Instead, he'd waited until she needed release as much as he did, and they'd come together as equals.

Equals? No! This creature belonged to his liege-lord! She was the enemy. She'd tried to kill him.

Sitting up, he tried to blanket himself in memories of when he'd wondered if the time spent around a Sakar woman-warrior might kill him. No enemy who'd tried to end him had lived. He'd never thought he'd have sex with one.

Never believed he'd let one take his cock in her mouth.

Denying his confusion, he grabbed her hands and hauled her to her feet with him. Still caught in sleep, she swayed, then straightened in the way of one who knows her life depends on always being alert.

"We travel today," he said.

She nodded but didn't ask for an explanation. After a moment, her gaze dropped to his morning-alert cock, but if she felt any superiority because he couldn't hide his arousal, she gave no indication. Neither did anything about her demeanor speak of what had happened between them.

As he did last night, he began by taking her outside so they could relieve themselves. Others were doing the same, but although his fellow warriors openly studied her, the slave-whores went to great lengths to ignore her. Wise in the way of the dull-witted creatures, he knew they could barely contain their curiosity. Probably most had never seen a woman-warrior.

Durc shook his penis dry and strode over. He boldly grabbed the captive's chin and forced her to look up at him. Mindful that a captive was the responsibility of every warrior, Bor made no move to make Durc release her.

"She smells of fucking," Durc said. "I heard her scream again, not the cry of a prisoner in pain but that of a woman getting what she craves."

"You had nothing better to do than listen to us?" Bor challenged.

"What do you expect? I had already satisfied my belly and this." He indicated his cock. "Tell me, War-liege. Is her pussy soft or is she a warrior even there?" Durc started to reach between the captive's legs. Cursing, she jumped back.

Bor had released her so she could tend to her needs. True, her wrists were still tied, but he half expected her to try to run. Instead, crouched and ready for attack, she faced Durc.

"Look at her!" Durc announced. "The bitch needs to be tamed. What is it, Captive?" he taunted. "You think your strength is equal to a Kebo warrior? How wrong you are. And how I relish teaching you the lesson." He made as if to grab her.

The captive took another backward step but continued to remind Bor of a trapped but unbeaten animal. He studied, not just the distance between them, but the lean, strong lines of her body. He'd deliberately kept her dressed because he didn't trust his reaction to her naked form but that would soon have to change. He'd always admired courage, even the courage of someone who'd tried to kill him.

"The lessons are mine," he reminded Durc. "She is my spoils, not yours."

"Until our liege-lord gets his hands on her," Durc shot back. "Then she will wish you had killed her."

The captive's eyes widened, but she gave no other indication that she'd heard. Not a muscle in her battle-honed body relaxed. *The next time we will fuck in daylight so I can watch.*

"Come here," he ordered, indicating the ground in front of him.

Her gaze flickered to Durc who was obviously enjoying the exchange.

"He will not touch you," Bor said. "Come here."

For maybe three breaths she remained where she was, looking free and trapped at the same time. Then, holding her head high, she did as he'd ordered. He closed his hand over her arm and led her back into the cave where the slave-whores were roasting meat and some roots. He pushed his captive toward a far corner of the large space so he could keep an eye on her while filling his belly. Soon the rest of the warriors had gathered around the morning fire and were passing the food between them, starting with him because he ranked highest. The slave-whores stood off to the side, their attention fixed on the meal because they were allowed to eat only once their masters had satisfied themselves.

Often captives were starved so they'd become so weak they offered little resistance, but although the others might expect him to break her down in this way, he wanted her strong. When the food came his way for the second time, he selected a little more for himself, then tore off a good-sized chunk of nearly raw meat and chose two small well-roasted roots. He threw those things in his captive's direction. They landed just out of her reach, but moving with a speed he knew not to ignore, she grabbed them and started eating.

"What are you doing?" Durc demanded. "I wanted that meat. The bitch does not deserve—"

"I will say this one time." He made sure he had everyone's attention. "This captive belongs to me. I bear the wound she inflicted. I brought her down. No one touches her unless I give permission, and no one speaks of what I should or should not do."

The others nodded acceptance. As for Durc—the younger, skilled but impulsive warrior only stared back. Not hurrying, Bor finished eating. Then he ordered the captive to come and stand in front of him. She did so, her attention divided between him and the nearby water-bladders. If he allowed her to drink out of them, it would be the act of an equal, but she was obviously thirsty. He ordered one of the slave-whores to pour some water into the captive's cupped hands, and although several of his fellow warriors laughed at the way she gulped and swallowed, he saw nothing amusing in her near desperation.

"Enough!" he said. "Captive, return to where you spent the night."

Straightening, she stared at him. In her gaze, he read not just gratitude for letting her drink but a look that said she believed he was treating her like an animal as a show for the others. But after what they'd shared in the night, he knew he'd never see her as an animal, a simple spoils of war.

Once she'd left, he turned his mind to the day's plans. Several warriors wanted to try to hunt down the Sakar who'd escaped, but he maintained that they risked walking into an ambush if they did. Instead, they'd return to the task Haddard had given them when they'd left the Kebo encampment five nights ago. The clan had been staying in the same place all through summer, but they needed to find an area capable of sustaining them through winter. Until yesterday's attack, they'd believed they'd found it here. Now they'd have to return to the low hills that had held earlier possibilities, for a closer look. With little discussion, the others agreed with him. Even Durc, who lived for battle, admitted that the crisp nights served as vivid reminders of how soon the weather would change. After many, many seasons of roaming far from the great valley, Haddard had declared that the time had come for the Kebo to take from the valley's riches, and from clans such as the Sakar that tried to lay claim to it. Although he didn't understand his liege-lord's decision, as his second-in-command, he'd committed himself to obeying.

Walking toward his captive, Bor acknowledged his conflicted emotions. He wanted to be alone with her again and learn more about her, to touch and allow himself to be touched. At the same time, he feared her power.

Fear? No!

Once his eyes had adjusted to the gloom, he spotted her standing in the middle of the small space. It occurred to him that she hadn't sat because she didn't know what to expect from him and needed to be ready. Immediately, those he'd just left no longer mattered. Instead, his world, his life, revolved around this small, soft, and strong creature.

"Tell me," he said in an attempt to distract himself from memories of how he'd lost himself inside her last night, "if we followed your warriors, would we find them waiting for us?"

The ghost of a smile flickered over her features. "If I said no, would you believe me? And if I said yes, would you believe that either?"

"You answered as I suspected. Do you understand why I fed you?"

"You want me strong."

He nodded but said nothing of why he wanted that. Maybe she didn't want to give voice to her thoughts either because she only watched him in that wild animal way he was becoming accustomed to.

He could have ordered one of the slave-whores to prepare her for travel, but if he did, she might think he was afraid to touch her. Never! He'd teach her who wielded the real power and when the lesson had been learned, she'd never think they might be equals. She'd become what she was, a prize and the spoils of war.

Chapter Eight

"Come here."

He'd ordered her like this before, and as she'd done earlier, Nuwaa obeyed. Even as she took the few necessary steps, she acknowledged the silent message beneath what each of them was doing. Bor was the victor. In that role, he commanded his world and possessions. She might fight him. Everything she'd been trained for since childhood screamed to do so. But if she did, it would be an act of instinct when only reason would keep her alive.

Unwilling to fill herself with thoughts of why she needed to stay alive, she looked up at him. She felt his warmth around her, seeping through the defenses of her flesh to touch lonely places. Last night, fucking him, she'd ceased to be alone. For those too-brief moments she'd been part of another human being, of this enemy.

His rough fingers on her bonds forced the admission to a secret corner of her mind. Once he'd untied her wrists, she rubbed them but continued to watch him. Suddenly he grabbed her around the waist and spun her away from him. With an effort, she kept her arms at her sides. She felt him working on the laces that kept her skirt in place, then the sharp downward tug. Eyes hot, she concentrated on the slide of softened material over her hips, thighs, calves. He left her skirt puddled around her ankles and ordered her to step out of it.

She'd been expecting this moment since she'd regained consciousness, but although he'd lifted her skirt during the night, being stripped naked from the waist down left her feeling diminished. Clothes were protection against the weather and symbols of one's status. Clothes kept private, parts of her body that could turn against her. Now every Kebo could see.

When he gripped her shirt hem and pulled it upward, she didn't try to fight but raised her arms and leaned forward. Fighting this particular act of domination would turn her into a primitive creature, and she wasn't going to allow him his superiority. He must have known what she was thinking because once he'd stripped her naked, he stepped back, folded his arms across his chest and studied her. She didn't know what to do with her hands so alternated between leaving them at her sides and trying to position them so her fingers hid her mons.

"No," he ordered. Grabbing her wrists yet again, he lifted her arms up and out away from her body. He released her and stepped back again, the unspoken message in the way he'd positioned her. She expected him to order her to reveal her pussy to him, but he merely went back to studying her. Her arms grew tired. She hated him.

"Enough," he said. She wasn't sure whether he was talking to himself or her but took the word as permission to assume a more comfortable position. No sooner had she lowered her arms than he reached down for the ropes he'd taken off her in the night. He began by wrapping a rope around her waist several times. Once he was satisfied with his work, he pulled first one hand and then the other to the front and secured them to the waist rope. Because he'd secured her like this before, she tried to tell herself he was done with her. Then he knotted yet another rope to the waist bonds and briefly let twin strands dangle between her legs. "Turn around," he ordered.

Her legs trembled a little as she did as he'd commanded.

"Spread."

No!

"Spread!"

Sweat broke out under her arms and down her back, but because she knew she had no choice, she complied. Once her legs were separated, he reached between them and grabbed the rope. Drawing out his intention, he slowly positioned the twin strands against her crotch before securing the rope by looping it through the waist rope at the small of her back. The rough strands pressed against her folds. She tried to tell herself the sudden letting down of her sex juices was simply an instinctive attempt to protect herself there, but she knew the truth. The invasion had turned her on.

When she tried to close her legs, he stopped her by pressing against the inside of her thighs. Her muscles trembled as he explored the rope's positioning, and she caught her breath when he tightened the cords a little more. She felt as if her lips and clit were being pressed up inside her.

He'd done this to her! He!

Her fury fell away as he started stroking her hips. Over and over again he slid his fingers over her naked flesh. Unable to stop herself, she let her head fall back. It came to rest on his shoulder, and he snaked an arm around her breasts to pull her against him. Shaking, she remained sealed to him. A hand now covered a breast while he continued to stroke her thigh. His cock grew and became insistent and demanding between them. Panting, she forgot everything except this. Him. Her legs felt as if they were melting. It didn't matter whether she clamped them together or left them splayed.

"Mine," she thought she heard him mutter but couldn't be sure.

Mine? Maybe.

Suddenly afraid of his domination over her emotions, she threw herself forward. At first he tried to keep her with him, then thrust her away with such force that she stumbled and struck the wall. By the time she'd regained her balance and whirled toward him, he'd picked up yet another rope.

"No!" she yelled. "Is this not enough!"

"Silence, Captive. Whatever I want to do to you, I will."

No!

Propelled by an instinct that went deeper and was more primitive than any she'd ever known, she tried to run around him toward the opening that meant freedom. But he was faster, grabbing her shoulders and throwing her to the ground. She landed on her side and managed to get on her back before he dropped beside her.

When she realized he intended to place the rope around her neck, she tried to kick him. Her struggles caused the crotch rope to grind against sensitive flesh. While she struggled to decrease the discomfort, he easily placed a noose around her.

"You will not fight me!"

"I am not an animal!"

"Aren't you?" He tugged on the crotch rope. Instant pain and heat flooded her. She felt a heartbeat away from a climax and couldn't stop the groan that erupted from her throat. He let up, then tugged again, and she wailed. "Not an animal?" he asked.

Feeling trapped, she put all her self-control into not fighting him. Teeth clenched, she ordered her muscles to relax, and although she continued to tremble, she succeeded in getting her legs to stop their erratic jerks.

"The captive fights herself," he observed. He continued to hold onto the crotch rope but was no longer torturing her with it. "Listen to me. The Kebo know how to make their female slaves loyal. We do not need ropes on our longtime whores because we have taught them that compliance brings reward. A whore hungry for satisfaction does what she can to earn her master's approval. You will learn. And when the lessons are complete, you will willingly spread your legs whenever I tell you to."

"I am not a slave! I am a warrior!"

"Are you?" He tugged. At the same time, he slid his free hand over her hot and hungry nether lips. "Tell me, *warrior*. Would you rather have your knife or my cock at this moment?"

Your cock! Your cock. "I will kill you!"

"Perhaps." He released the rope pressure but kept his hand in place. "But not today."

* * * * *

Her captor had placed the crotch rope so it moved when she did. She was grateful that it didn't grind against her and irritate her flesh, but she couldn't for a moment dismiss its presence. In truth, a hunger that had nothing to do with the state of her stomach now gnawed between her legs. He'd made her a prisoner, not of the enemy but her own body. Not only couldn't she escape her humming need, she couldn't do anything to satisfy it. Although having to walk with her hands positioned in front of her was awkward, she was careful not to move them because that only increased the burning on sensitive and too-alive skin.

What was it he'd said...that the Kebo knew how to keep their whores hungry for sex. She wasn't a whore! She was a warrior.

Sex-starved and helpless.

Bor had turned her over to one of the slave-whores who kept a firm grip on the neck rope as they followed the warriors along a small, meandering creek. The other women were naked which perhaps should have made her feel less exposed, but it didn't. Their value within the Kebo stemmed from their bodies, while always before, her worth had been dependant upon her weapons, bravery, and fighting skill. Being reduced to a physical creature both infuriated and shamed her which was surely what Bor had intended. At least none of the men were, at present, observing her discomfort, although going by her constantly dripping pussy, discomfort was a lie.

"Where are you from?" she asked the big-breasted, narrow-hipped, light brown-haired woman walking just ahead of her. "How long have you been a prisoner of the Kebo?"

The woman didn't answer, but Nuwaa read her reaction in her suddenly lifted head, so repeated her question. "Where are you from? I have seen your hair color only on traders and other travelers."

"I have not been given permission to speak to you," the woman muttered.

"Did he forbid you?"

"No."

"Then it must not matter to him."

"Please, I do not want him to be angry at me."

"Why? What would he do?"

That seemed to stump the woman who kept looking back over her shoulder. Thinking the woman might stumble, Nuwaa drew alongside her. The crotch rope continued to make its presence known and threatened to distract her from what might be a vital conversation. "Would he punish you?" she prompted.

"Punish? Not War-liege Bor. These days he does not concern himself with such things but…"

"But what?"

The woman looked around at the others. Then, perhaps satisfied that no one could overhear, she said, "The other whores and I eat when it pleases our masters. We sleep when they say we can. Some of our masters are quick to anger and punish."

And being at the Kebo warriors' mercy has broken your spirit. In the past, the lives of slaves had been of little concern to her. Now ropes and nudity had all but turned her into one of them.

"You were captured?" she asked, thinking to change the subject so hopefully the woman would relax a little.

"Traded. I was born a slave in my birth tribe. When I became old enough to have value, they sold me."

She spoke so matter-of-factly that Nuwaa hurt for the creature who'd never known or expected freedom.

"So the Kebo bought you," she mused. "I have always heard that Kebo warriors captured those they intended to use as whores."

"Most of the time they do." Enthusiasm entered the woman's voice for the first time. Obviously she enjoyed sharing a bit of gossip. "Kebo warriors love to hunt for new slave-whores. Sometimes it seems they would rather do that than defend and protect their clan."

"Turning a woman into a slave-whore excites them?" The question forced her to concentrate on the ropes controlling her body. She couldn't say without reservation that confining her in this matter would make Bor fuck-hungry, but it wouldn't surprise her. She didn't want to think about tonight.

"They are men. They think with their cocks." The woman chuckled. "Their liege-lord, Haddard, lives to fuck. He wants a woman with him always, sometimes taking her several times in a single day. In my birth clan, the liege was ancient and ill, no longer ruled by his cock. His warriors had whores, but they did not fuck in public or frequently."

"In other words, because Haddard is the way he is, his warriors feel free to act like animals in heat."

"Sometimes. Sometimes they wear out their cocks because they believe that is how they must act so their liege-lord will see them as men." She chuckled again. "Men do not know how much they reveal while they are between a woman's legs."

The woman's insight caused Nuwaa to fall silent. To her own lord, nothing had greater importance than making other clans understand that the Sakar were superior to all others. Constant readiness for fighting took precedence over everything else, even providing food and shelter. She'd always shared Radislay's belief, but now she asked herself if there might be other priorities. She'd never place fucking first because the needs of babies and children took precedence.

"The whores who are captured, do they ever try to run away?" she asked.

"I have seen it, but not for a long time."

"Why not?"

For the first time, the other woman really looked at her. Nuwaa saw a flicker of something that might be sympathy, but then it faded. "Because they know what will happen if they failed. Besides—" She ran her free hand over her body. "I am naked and unarmed. Where would I go? How would I survive?"

You'd know how if you were a warrior. "What if all the whores decided to run at the same time? If you fled as one, you would have strength."

"We would starve."

"Not a single whore knows how to hunt?"

"Men hunt, not women."

"Perhaps not among the Kebo, but in other clans such as mine, some women are trained as warriors and hunters. Surely the Kebo have captured a few of those before me."

"Yes."

"What happened?"

It took a while but the woman finally explained that a number of seasons ago a trio of women-warriors from a clan she didn't know the name of, had been captured in a raid and brought before Liege-lord Haddard. He'd raped them repeatedly and, after he was done with them, had turned them over to his warriors. One of the women had gotten hold of a knife and had killed herself with it. Another, handed from warrior to warrior, was dead after two nights. The third lived through the winter but tried to escape in the spring. She'd been caught and hauled in front of Liege-lord Haddard who'd ordered her tortured.

"Bor was not here when the woman escaped but returned while she was being tortured. He said nothing but stepped up to her and cut her throat."

"He what?" Nuwaa felt cold.

"She was half-dead," the woman whispered. "Even if he'd stopped what the others were doing to her, she would not have lived. I thank him for his kindness."

Nuwaa could barely concentrate. Her liege-lord had made it clear that the Kebo were savages, but to deliberately set about to slowly kill someone for wanting back her freedom was beyond her comprehension. The Sakar killed those who sought to kill them. They took slaves, but they did not seek revenge on those slaves.

"Does Haddard hate Bor for what he did?"

"No. Haddard praised Bor, saying a man capable of leading men into battle makes his own decisions. Then Bor declared that there would be no more torturing of captives unless he orders it."

"Haddard agreed?"

"He must have. No one questions what the Kebo liege-lord does because his guidance comes from the gods."

"There have been no more women-warriors taken prisoner since those three?"

"Not until you. That must be because there are so few of them."

The reminder forced Nuwaa's thoughts back on herself. The whole time she'd been probing for what information she could, her body had continued to respond to the ropes pressing against her woman-place. Like too-long denied sex, the pressure made it nearly impossible for her to concentrate on anything else. If she'd thought the other woman had a measure of courage, she would have begged her to at least loosen the crotch tie and finger her until she experienced the release she now longed for as much as she'd craved water earlier.

When this endless day was over, would her captor take pity on her and spill his seed inside her, or would he find other ways to prove his mastery of her, perhaps even increasing her frustration? Questions about how much more sexual tension she might have to endure nearly forced a groan from her. By turn she tried to rub her nub against the strands or struggled to pull her pussy up inside her and away from the sweet torture. Neither attempt worked. She felt exhausted and desperate at the same time.

"You are silent," the woman said. She gave the noose a faint tug. "Experiencing."

"Yes," Nuwaa admitted.

"I understand."

"You do?"

"Being naked and without the skills to survive without a man to hunt for us is not the only reason I and the other slave-whores stay with the warriors."

They'd been walking on flat land where soft grass covered the ground, but were approaching a rocky area. Despite the upcoming need to concentrate more fully on her footing, Nuwaa knew she didn't dare let this conversation end yet. "What do they do to you?" she asked.

The woman stopped and reached between Nuwaa's legs. Cupping rope and crotch, she pressed. "This. Making us so hungry that nothing except an end to the hunger matters. When it pleases them, they turn us into animals." After briefly rubbing Nuwaa's swollen lips, she placed her juice-drenched fingers in her own mouth. "This will please Bor. He wants you weak, not strong."

* * * * *

The runner Bor had sent ahead to the rest of the clan, found them just after the approaching night put an end to the day's travel. Despite a successful deer kill earlier, Bor had kept his warriors on the move as long as he dared. While looking out for more game and taking careful note of the area's other riches, he'd been able to at least partly distract himself from what might happen once he was alone with his captive again. Now, however, listening to what the runner had brought back from Liege-lord Haddard, he felt his belly tighten.

"I am glad our liege-lord is pleased," he said because it was expected of him.

"Of course he is," Durc interjected. "Our liege-lord has been like a wolf after prey with his constant talk about proving Kebo superiority over the Sakar. And to know that we are bringing him a woman-warrior must bring him great pleasure. Tell us?" he asked the runner. "Did he masturbate while you were telling him?"

Grinning, the runner vigorously nodded. Then he turned his attention back to Bor. "Our liege-lord wants you to return now, not wait until you have finished scouting this area."

Although he'd expected that, Bor's tension increased. "Did he say anything else about the captive?"

"She is to be kept alive. Not injured."

It wasn't I who destroyed that other captive. I simply ended her suffering.

"What else?" Durc interjected. "Certainly he does not expect our war-liege to keep his cock out of his prize."

"No." The runner looked uneasy. "But he said…"

"What?" Bor demanded.

"You are to think of her only as a prisoner, not a warrior. She is the spoils, nothing more."

It is already too late for that.

Despite the risk to his heated body, Bor looked around until he spotted the cluster of slave-whores standing a respectful distance from the conversation they knew they had no right to. In the rapidly fading light he easily spotted the taller, straighter, darker figure of his captive. She was looking at him.

Remember, she is a captive. Nothing more.

"If you cannot follow our liege-lord's orders," Durc taunted, "turn her over to me. I see nothing but a cunt."

It took all Bor's self-control not to throw his fellow warrior to the ground. "I took her, not you." He spoke loudly enough so everyone heard. "If you touch her, it will be an act of defiance against my leadership. Are you ready to do that?"

Durc made an elaborate show of shrugging off the challenge, but Bor understood that more than Durc's desire to prove himself had been behind his words. The handsome captive had obviously wrapped her spell around more than one Kebo man.

After telling the others that they'd start back home in the morning, he dismissed them for the evening. Because they'd been on their feet all day, most would be content to sit and watch while the slave-whores prepared the meal. As for him, he was expected to take control of his prize. Not sure what he would do, he walked toward her. Someone had already gathered wood and started the cooking fire, which provided the light he both needed and dreaded.

The tethered woman-warrior again studied his every move. If he thought the time she'd spent being sexually teased would strip her of some of her defiance, he was mistaken. Even as she sought to cross one leg in front of the other, she glared at him. Glaring back, he grabbed the neck lead from the slave-whore.

"She is ripe," the woman said, her head downcast as if hoping for his approval. "I have been testing her."

"I did not expect it to be otherwise." He gave the whore a shove in the direction of the fire.

Hands clasped in front of her, she scurried away.

"Her name is Basaw," his captive said. "She has never known freedom. Think on that, War-liege Bor. Ask yourself what it is like to feel less than human from the moment of your birth."

Of all the things she could have said to him once they were alone again, he'd never thought it would be this. During unguarded moments he'd imagined that she'd drop to her knees and try to take his cock into her mouth, begging him through her behavior to end her unrelenting stimulation. However, despite the bright spots on her cheeks and sex smell, she'd retained control of her mind and body.

"Basaw," he heard himself say. "I did not know."

"Because she is not human to you." She paused. "Am I the same? Not your equal?"

How could she stand naked and tied before him and demand to be considered his equal? One look at the defiance blazing in her eyes, a moment of thought given to his still-sore side, and he had his answer. She'd been well-trained as a warrior.

"I do not know what you are," he admitted. "I have never known anyone like you."

"Neither have I," she whispered.

With her admission, something shifted. He'd just admitted a vulnerability he'd never sensed in himself before and certainly never thought he'd admit. Now she'd done the same. Saying nothing, he untied her hands and released the tension on her crotch. Never taking her eyes from him, she rubbed her wrists. She stood motionless as if not trusting her body. He slipped his hands between her legs. Her hot fluids drenched his fingers.

"Drink of me," she challenged. "Have no doubt of what you have done to me."

Because he had no choice, he placed his fingers in his mouth and tasted her. As her juices slid down his throat, he felt himself heat. His cock beneath his loincloth responded, and she noted his condition with a jerk of her head. "Are you pleased?" she asked. "You can call yourself a great warrior because you have been trained in the ways of a woman's body?"

He yanked her close with the neck rope. For an instant, she fought him, then, still meeting his gaze, she surrendered.

"Trained?" he asked.

"Basaw told me of what the men of the Kebo do to keep their slave-whores with them. How proud you must be! Why use ropes when a woman can be controlled by her cunt?" She fingered the strands around her throat. "Surely you believe that in a few suns you will no longer need this on me because I will follow you around on hands and knees, sniffing your ass and whimpering as I spread myself."

It took all his self-control not to hit her. Then, even as he ordered himself not to allow anger to rule him, he understood what lay behind her words.

"Perhaps you want to make a wager," he said. "You say you are a warrior so surely you believe you can stand up to whatever I do to you. As long as your heart beats, you will not become my whore."

She blinked but gave no other indication of her reaction.

"I say that after three nights and days you will have forgotten everything except me and my command of you."

"How? By depriving me of food and water? By making me walk with a rope against my cunt?" She shook her head. "You do not understand what it is to be a Sakar warrior. You never will."

A warrior? At that moment he saw only a woman's naked and accessible body, great dark eyes that might haunt him for the rest of his life.

"No starvation. No unrelenting thirst," he told her.

* * * * *

Even as she accepted a small basket of stew and a full water-bladder from Basaw, Nuwaa's thoughts remained on Bor. Maybe she should have, but she'd made no effort to hide her thirst and hunger from him. Besides, he too was drinking as if he couldn't get enough. It occurred to her that he was making a statement by eating with her instead of ordering her to wait until he was done like the slave-whores did and wondered what the other warriors thought.

They sat across from each other on the grass-covered ground with her neck rope tied to his wrist. Although it would have been more comfortable to sit cross-legged, she couldn't bring herself to expose her juncture to him and so rested her weight on her haunches. In contrast, he made no effort to spare her the sight of his still-erect cock. Although she could hear the others, she paid little attention to their firelit outlines.

She'd pushed him and risked his fury. But she had no choice because her life depended on learning everything she could about her captor. He hadn't struck her when she might have if things had been reversed between them. Neither had he immediately taken advantage of the sexual tension he'd planted deep and strong inside her. But he would. She had no doubt of it.

Will you force me to beg to be fucked?

Earlier she'd told him she'd die before she'd crawl on hands and knees to him, but the truth was, it took everything she had not to give into the need.

The hunger inside should have quieted by now. If he'd left her alone, the night air would have tamped down the flames. But he sat so close she felt him on her skin. Like a constantly fed fire, his presence lapped at her. She didn't know how much longer she could keep her hands off herself, off him. Her throat clogged with pleas to be fucked. Her fingers throbbed at the thought of housing him. And her pussy—

"Stand up."

Well-trained in obeying her liege-lord's commands, she was nearly on her feet before she realized what she'd done. By then it was too late because Bor was already standing. He gripped her shoulders to spin her away from him. She didn't fight as he tied her hands behind her before removing the ropes around her waist and over her crotch. "What are you doing?" she demanded.

"Bathing you."

He took her to the creek they'd been following, and after ordering her to kick off her shoes and doing the same himself, he ordered her to get into it. He kept pace, not pausing as he yanked off his loincloth and dropped it on the ground. Now he wore only his cougar-claw necklace. At the middle, the water barely reached her waist, but he forced her onto her knees, then bent her back until her legs began floating. If not for his hold on her, her head would have gone under. He held her by the back of her neck as the gently running water drenched her hair. Although she hated the loss of control, she loved having the sweat and grime of the past few days wash away. The moon provided scant illumination, but her senses told her everything she needed to know. Once again he held her life in his hands. If he'd wanted he could easily drown her.

She was still trying to get used to the awkward and precarious position when he set her back on her knees and untied the leather cord that had held her long braid in place. Wet clumps of hair now lay on her shoulders. Then she felt his fingers on her scalp and nearly lost herself in the both unwanted and wanted sensation as he brushed her hair free and loose. Again he dipped her back, and she imagined her hair floating on the surface.

When he was satisfied, he positioned her so her knees rested on the graveled creek bottom with water lapping at her throat and turned his attention to washing her face. He repeatedly cupped his hands and let the water run down from her scalp. It slid over her forehead, closed eyes, cheeks, finally trickling off her chin. She, who'd never been handled like this, had started shivering from anticipation and cold by the time he finished. Her nipples had hardened, a fact he brought to her attention by taking hold of them.

"You believe I will force you to offer yourself to me, but I say it will not be necessary. If I want, your body belongs to me, but it responds to more than ropes and cruelty."

Demonstrating, he pulled her toward him with nothing more than his grip on her nipples. She tried to resist, but her knees slipped out from under her. She would have fallen face-first into the water if he hadn't caught her. This time when he righted her, she knew that no matter how much she hated his touch, she had no choice but to stand and endure.

Endure gentle caresses on my shoulders, his fingertips massaging my breasts, palms stroking my sides and hips, scant pressure against the inside of my thighs telling me to spread my legs? No, not endure. Losing myself in the sensual treatment.

"Where is your fight, Captive?" he asked. "You still have use of your legs. Run. Run and show me you do not want this."

She bit down and struggled not to let her head loll back while he bathed her mons, lips, slit. Even with the cold, she jumped every time he ran a nail over her clit. After what seemed like forever, he'd finished with her cunt and sank to his knees so he could concentrate on her legs. Even tied and helpless, it felt wrong to be standing while he crouched beneath her. From the first moment she'd seen him, his greater size and strength had made its impact. She tried to imagine him as her prisoner, but the image wouldn't hold.

Finally, he forced her onto her knees again. She waited where he'd positioned her while he cleaned himself. The moon presented her with the shadow of a man intent on his own needs, a man who had dismissed her but left her where she had to remain part of his world. If she hadn't become so cold, she might have begged him to let her bathe him. As it was, she was becoming numb, the sexual flames somehow still crackling beneath the surface.

"Simple things," he said. "Taste upon taste upon taste until your appetite for my touch dominates."

"I hate you."

Instead of calling her on the lie, he pulled her to her feet. Instead of letting her stand, however, he gripped her by the waist and pushed her back. Her floating legs touched his, and although he now held her securely by her elbows, she wrapped her legs around his hips. She felt his cock against her just out of reach of her hungry core. Water supported her, and she wondered if she might stay like this forever. Yes, she was afraid of drowning, but that wasn't the only emotion. Her legs hugged him, growing stronger and stronger, insistent.

"Your mind may hate me, Captive. But your body does not."

Not trusting herself to speak, she imagined him repositioning her so the intimate union could be made. If she hadn't been so cold, her imagination might have been her undoing.

"You tremble," he said. "If I keep you in here, the fires will go out, and I do not want that."

As she silently thanked him, he lifted her out of the water and carried her to the shore. She expected him to put her down, but he walked with her back to the place he'd chosen for them to spend the night. She fought the chilled air the only way she could by pressing herself against his chest. No man had ever carried her. She'd never expected the experience to make her feel as one with a male.

He lay her down on thick fur with her bound hands under her and covered her with a similar layer before drying her with it. As with the washing, he drew out the act, touching her everywhere, lingering where she was most sensitive. When he pressed her legs together and slid his hands over them, she moaned under her breath. Then he rested the heels of both hands on her mons, and she opened herself to him. He warmed his fingers against her pussy, and she moaned louder and ground her buttocks against the earth.

"Forced?" he whispered.

"No," she admitted because her body didn't know how to lie.

Chapter Nine

When Bor removed the rope from her neck and followed that by turning her over and freeing her hands, Nuwaa kicked the fur off her legs but didn't try to look up at him. She now lay on her side facing away from him. Everything about her lengthy warrior training screamed at her to keep her eyes on him, but she knew all too well the risk of seeing his body. Legs tucked up against her belly, she struggled to sort out the pieces of what had happened since they'd stopped walking. Although she was grateful for her full belly and clean skin, those things barely made an impact.

She'd deliberately thrown cutting words at him in an attempt to place emotional distance between them and hoped the sight of her back continued to carry that message, but maybe, probably, he'd seen through the lies.

He'd touched her in ways she'd never been touched, tested her far beyond her experience, and he wasn't yet done with her. Maybe he wouldn't be satisfied until he'd destroyed everything she'd ever been.

I will not let it happen! I will kill us first.

But when he rolled her onto her back and knelt between her legs, she knew she'd told herself a lie.

"A woman is most alive here." He made his point by touching her clit. "Not here." He briefly slid a finger inside her. "For a man, a woman's cave is her most powerful place, but she is ruled by the entrance to that cave."

How do you know that? Who taught you —

"Our grandfathers and our grandfathers' grandfathers believed that only fucking brought their women pleasure, but our liege-lord's father was a man of great appetites and curiosity." His fingers were now all back outside her, resting warm and alive against her freely weeping core. She dug her fingers into the fur and fought to keep her buttocks still. "As a youth my lord began working with his birth clan's female captives. Bit by bit he learned their secrets. Once he had done that, he started teaching them things about themselves they did not know."

"How...how do you know this?"

He switched his grip to her hips so he could lift her legs up and onto his with her feet now behind him. Her buttocks rested on his thighs with her core open and accessible to him. He lay his hard cock against the apex between her thigh and labia. It twitched, and she nearly came from the sensation.

"Liege-lord Haddard learned at his father's side. But after his father died, he left his home and traveled alone for many moons while he became one with Lifelight. At length, Lifelight brought him to what are now, the Kebo, and taught them to believe in his power. He shared his fighting skills with those he chose as his warriors and selected the strongest and most intelligent females for them to breed with. We became travelers and takers from those who are weaker. Along with weapons and food, we began turning some of the female captives into slave-whores. Our liege-lord guided his warriors in the ways of drawing loyalty out of those creatures."

And you are his war-liege, his most prized pupil. And I am your captive.

Instead of being revolted, she simply panted as he stroked her mons almost as a mother strokes a child. Against all reason and training, she felt cared for, even prized. Giving up on her earlier determination to keep her hands off him, she lay her hands over what of his thighs she could reach and started massaging him. He made a sound she'd never heard before, not the groan of an aroused man, gentler, less sure. Wondering about its meaning, she increased the contact and stared up at him. He was looking down at her, his mood hidden by the night. But although neither could see into the heart and soul of the other, she felt as if she'd become part of him.

His fingers glided over her belly and the scant layers of flesh over her pelvic bone. Again and again he kissed her flesh with his, always coming back to her wet and sensitive pussy. Her throat, which still retained the feel of the rope he'd placed around it, felt hot. She breathed through an open mouth and gave away everything by urgently moving her buttocks. If he chose, he could easily rope her again. Tonight at least there was no escape.

Fuck me! Please. Make us one.

Despite the red haze her world had become, she felt the first touch of his cock against her opening. His organ slid in as if he'd been born and bred to fit there, but instead of burying himself deep and full, he stopped with his tip just past her lips. She felt the promise but not the fulfillment.

"Take," she begged. "Please."

"Soon. Soon. Soon."

Once he'd settled his tip securely inside her slippery home, he used his fingers to close her wet folds around him. Gently, so gently that at first she wasn't sure, his cock moved. Maybe she could have concentrated on that sensation alone if at the same time he hadn't started rubbing her labia from side to side. He rocked into her, drew back slightly, rocked forward again. All the while he continued to stimulate her folds. Her pussy wept. She couldn't begin to comprehend his self-control.

"All of you. Now!" she begged.

"Feel me. Continue to press your fingers into me because that is how I judge your journey."

She became water heated by a summer sun, a leaf caught in a swirling wind. In her mind, she fought the wind and hid from the sun, but he'd turned her mind into nothing. She lived for him. Existed for him. Waited for his gift and great strength.

By fragmented bits she realized that something had changed. Not only had he stopped caressing her opening with his cock, but he no longer had hold of her.

"Sit up," he whispered. "Then get on your hands and knees."

If he'd told her to run naked into a winter storm, at that moment she would have obeyed, so presenting her ass to him with her upper body supported by her forearms was easy. She felt her fluids run down her inner thighs. Although she understood the danger, she looked over her shoulder at him as he positioned himself behind her. Desperately eager to accommodate him, she pushed her buttocks toward him and increased her stance. This time he made no effort to stop with his cock just at her entrance but presented her with all of him in a smooth, strong thrust.

The promise of an end to unrelenting sexual frustration poured over her. She felt herself begin to come, but as the first wave slammed into her, she struggled to resist. Tonight she didn't want a fast, hard climax. She needed to relish the release, needed to experience the man responsible so she might, eventually, understand him and her response to him and defend herself against him.

Much as she longed to hold him, something she'd never imagined wanting, she concentrated on his hands on her buttocks and his organ filling her. His cock kissed her inner length and set off lightning strikes wherever he pressed. No wonder she'd always enjoyed fucking this way.

Besides, she reminded herself as their mating became everything, it was better for him to be only a sex partner, her equal in matters of the flesh.

Empowered by her decision, she simply existed as thrust after thrust enveloped her. Her pussy burned, wept, growing, growing and becoming her entire existence. Behind her closed eyes she *saw* him crouched at her entrance. He'd become a slave to her offering just as she was a slave to the sensations he'd created in her. For these moments when they no longer existed as separate human beings, they owned each other. They might have only a single thing in common, but right now it was enough.

Her breasts hung hot and heavy, swaying with the rhythm he'd created. She breathed to his beat, heated and splintered. Dimly she heard his urgent animal sounds that said the day's anticipation had been equally long for him.

She felt him start to come, felt his hard release. *I do this for you*, she thought as she braced herself to weather his urgency. *My gift to you so you will never forget my strength.*

Then the gift turned inward. The explosion she'd managed to hold back became more than she could control. Sobbing loudly, she dove into it. She felt her cunt muscles close down around him and heard their joined cries. Then nothing.

* * * * *

Bor pulled the woman against him and lay down. They smelled of sweat and sex. She felt feverish, but so did he. She was so limp he briefly wondered if she was unconscious, then decided she hadn't yet found her way back. He rested on his side with her cradled against him, her back and buttocks sealed to his chest and pelvis. His cock had become a useless organ, but even as the need to sleep dragged at him, he knew it wouldn't be long before it came back to life. If he put distance between himself and this powerful sexual creature who'd invaded his world, he could keep his cock dormant, but he didn't want to.

They'd sleep. Then they'd wake, maybe as one, and feed off each other again.

Reaching around her, he cupped a hand over a breast and housed and sheltered it. Only when she covered his hand with her own fingers did he acknowledge that he hadn't placed any ropes back on her. He should because his liege-lord would accept nothing less than having her thus delivered to him. But he'd never wanted to spend the entire night with a woman before. Now he did because she'd become his equal in so many ways.

"I will not run," she whispered as if reading his mind.

He wanted to know why she'd made that promise. At the same time, he believed they should never touch certain subjects. When she said nothing else, he listened to her breathing and felt her flesh against his and let sleep coat him.

A dream stole over him. At first he was aware of nothing except thick fog. He was trying to walk in the fog but could barely see where he was going. Feeling claustrophobic, he stopped and waited for his eyes to adjust. After a short while, he thought he saw movement so concentrated on it. Whatever it was came closer, closer.

His captive.

She seemed to be clothed in layers of white fog that slid over her, teasing him with glimpses of breasts and hips. Then she smiled, the gentle gesture soft as spring sun. He'd never seen her smile, never heard her laugh, but he did now. The sound reminded him of morning birds. He reached for her, but his hand found no substance.

"Perhaps I am not real," she told him. "Only a dream for a lonely man."

"Why have you come to me?"

Because you are not the only one who is lonely.

Accepting that he'd tapped into her thoughts, he stepped closer. She seemed to be taking on substance, but because he was afraid she might disappear, he didn't try to touch her again. She stood before him, floated really, a cloud.

I did not know I was lonely, he told her in his mind. *Not until you came into my life.*

Neither did I.

She'd stopped smiling. He thought he saw her eyes mist over but maybe it was only the fog. *What do you want?* he asked.

I do not know. Something I have never felt before.

It is the same for me.

* * * * *

Sometime in the silent stretch between night and morning, he woke to discover her shivering and trying to warm herself on his chest. Because he too was cold, he covered them with a pelt. Then she stirred, and although he couldn't see her features, he knew she was looking at him.

I had a dream, he wanted to tell her. *We both said things no other human has ever heard.* But he knew better.

He wanted to kiss her. He, who'd never thought of kissing the whores who accompanied the warriors, needed to feel her mouth on his in the way of Kebo men and women who'd found those they intended to spend their lives with.

Instead, he took her breast in his mouth and filled himself with it. She moaned and pressed her legs against his and wrapped her arms around him. Her touch both weakened him and made him want to shout with joy. The slave-whores stroked him because it was their mission and purpose. It was different with her, and although he couldn't comprehend the emotion that drove her to experience his flesh, he accepted the gift.

He sucked on her breast and ran his arm between her legs so she lifted one and placed it over his hip, then moved toward her so his cock felt her moist opening. This time when he entered her, their mouths were so close he felt her every breath.

They rocked together, their bodies like twin drumbeats. She might have touched her lips to his but by then his thunderous climax was upon him. She cried out as she had before, her sudden, strong release matching his.

As he fell asleep again, he held her.

* * * * *

Bor was still sleeping when Nuwaa slipped out from under the covers. Taking advantage of the new day, she looked down at the man. Last night's memories remained just out of reach, and she kept them there because she wasn't yet awake enough to deal with them.

Golden hair clung to his cheek. His lashes were slightly darker. Although his muscles were at rest, his strength remained evident. He had lean hips and long, powerful legs, the body of a warrior. The body of a man made for fucking.

Feeling her nipples harden, she cupped them and thought of the sensation when he'd taken one in his mouth. It hadn't occurred to her to wonder if he might bite her, not because sexual need's grip had been too powerful for other thought, but because she trusted him.

She was still dealing with the admission when he opened his eyes. There was nothing slow about his awakening. He dealt with it in the same way she always had, instantly alert.

"I will not run," she told him as he was sitting up. *Not now at least.*

He studied her a moment. "I believe you."

Not touching, they walked together to the creek, and although her teeth were chattering by the time she'd finished bathing herself, she didn't hurry because cold water quieted some of the heat ignited by nothing more than his gaze. Perhaps he'd had the same thought because although his cock had been erect when he stepped into the water, it had relaxed by the time he reached shore again.

"I heard you," someone said. Turning from Bor, she recognized Durc who was walking toward them. "Heard both of you, not once but twice." He jerked his head at her. "No ropes?"

"No," was all Bor said.

"The captive has already become a slave to your cock?"

Bor grunted, then started walking back toward the encampment. She kept pace. Although she expected Durc to say more, he didn't which gave her too much time to ponder his question. Had she indeed become her captor's sex slave? *No!* echoed through her, but she knew it was a lie.

Bor was changing her in ways she couldn't comprehend. All she knew was, she would rather die than end this journey to understanding. Even now with her pussy still swollen and sensitive from last night's fucking, she longed to have him fill her again. Her flesh ached with the need for his touch, his fingers stroking her. Her breasts belonged in his hands and mouth. She wanted to feel his fingers on her throat and know he would never hurt her and was only trying to feel the blood pulsing through her veins.

Flames of desire took hold of her. Always before, her arousal had been limited to her pussy. As soon as a man had spilled himself inside her and she'd climaxed, she'd been eager to regain her own space. Now for the first time in her life, she wanted to share the same air with another human being, with the warrior who was taking her to the Kebo village where she'd try to kill his liege-lord and probably die in the aftermath.

When they reached their sleeping place, Bor reached into the pack a slave-whore had been carrying for him and pulled out her clothes. "I want you walking beside me today," he said as he handed them to her. "I want to learn if a Sakar warrior looks at her world in the same way a Kebo does."

His equal.

Although she knew that wasn't true, she gratefully put on the simple garments that set her apart from the slave-whores. At the same time she wished she could spend more time with the women as she tried to learn why they accepted the way they were treated. True, Bor had expertly prepared her body for sex yesterday, but once that fire had been extinguished, she'd still wanted to fuck him. From what she understood of the slave-whores, they cared nothing about their masters, and yet they willingly spread their legs whenever one commanded. To go through life with so little thought, so little emotion—

"I have never been here before," she admitted, because questions about what ruled a slave-whore were making her anxious for answers that might never come. "But you have?"

"Yes, during summer."

"Is it different from where the Kebo are staying?"

He told her that the land where they'd been camped wasn't as level. There was abundant water and even more important, the area was rich with wildlife. Countless birds lived around a large lake filled with fat fish.

"Why are the Kebo not already here if this is where you wish to spend winter?" she asked.

"Because where we now are is abundant." He paused. "And there are no abuli there."

Abuli were the size of small bears but much faster with a cougar's ability to move silent and unseen until they attacked. Meat-eaters and extremely aggressive, they were equally at home on the ground and in trees. They had massive jaws filled with two rows of sharp teeth and long claws that could lay open a man's chest with a single swipe. The first abuli she'd seen was a dead one brought to the village when she was a child. She remembered the celebration that had followed the telling of how the abuli had attacked a group of hunters who'd managed to bury all their spears in it while it tore at the fresh deer carcass they'd been gutting. Fortunately, the abuli had been more interested in the meat than chasing after the hunters who'd immediately scattered.

She and the other warriors-in-training had been allowed to come close so they could touch the dead teeth and fangs. Although her size had nearly doubled since then, and she'd seen a number of them from a distance and fashioned her weapons from the bones of a dead one she'd come across, she remembered her sense of awe and fear as the hunters told of the abuli's speed, the length of its leaps, how quickly it had torn the carcass apart.

"Why do you want to live where there are abuli?" she asked.

"Because Liege-lord Haddard's dreams say this is where we will spend the winter," he said. "And because he believes the abulis' presence will keep other clans away."

He went on to explain that they planned to build a fence around the cluster of *mogans* where the Kebo intended to live. In addition, they'd keep captured hyenas around because the small, timid creatures could smell an abuli coming and signal a warning. She admired the Kebo's resourcefulness and willingness to abide by their leader's wishes, but if she was their lord, she'd wait until she had another dream.

"Do you know how many abuli are here?" she asked.

"Only a few. They are loners and each claims its own territory. Once we have killed them, even the smallest child will be safe. But our enemies will not know what we have done. They will continue to fear the beasts."

"How will you know when they are all dead? I want my spear," she said. "If an abuli attacks, I need to be a warrior."

"And maybe you will use your spear to try to kill me."

"Do you believe that?"

He answered by picking up her spear and handing it to her. Gripping it again made her feel strong and whole. At the same time, she understood how much trust his gesture represented. *If only he knew.*

He covered her hand with his so they were equally responsible in holding the weapon. "I understand about the abuli, but it isn't the only reason you believe you should be a warrior again."

She couldn't tell him she needed to stay with him so she could complete her mission. "My liege-lord has always said the Kebo are our enemy, but his words are no longer enough. I need to understand—"

"Would you feel that way if I had not captured you?"

After a moment she shook her head. She longed to ask him to put his arms around her so, maybe, she'd understand the look in his eyes, but she didn't dare because she'd already risked so much being around him. She no longer knew where he ended and she began.

"I do not know your name," he said.

"Nuwaa."

* * * * *

Nuwaa wasn't *Captive*. Nuwaa spoke of a girl being named by whoever had raised her, a warrior-in-training, a valued member of her clan, a fighter, an equal.

He'd deliberately turned her over to a slave-whore yesterday because he hadn't wanted to be close to her, but so much had changed between them since then. As they walked to where the warriors were gathering, he struggled to comprehend everything that had changed, but the possibilities overwhelmed him. If she tried to run, he'd chase and recapture her. If she raised her weapon against him or the others, he might have to kill her. But as long as she matched her steps to his and her eyes too scanned their surroundings for danger, they were equals.

And tonight—

"What is this?" Durc indicated Nuwaa. "Has she stolen your senses along with your cock?"

"There are now enough eyes to look for the abuli," he said. "She is a warrior."

"A captive! A hostage. A taker of our war-liege's cock."

Both because Durc's taunt enraged him and because maybe the other warrior was right, he turned to the rest of the men. "I say I will walk with her. Who among you will not?"

Obviously thrown off balance by the question, the others exchanged glances. Then Rasja who would soon be too old to carry a warrior's weapons but would still be valued for his wisdom stepped forward. "I saw her fight," he said. "Even when she was tied and helpless, she showed no fear. She is a warrior."

"A Sakar!" Durc spat.

"Maybe no longer," Rasja countered. "She carries our war-liege's seed in her. Perhaps it has changed her."

By the way the others were nodding, Bor knew the situation had been resolved to their satisfaction. What Rasja's argument had failed to answer was how much of her was now inside him.

Fortunately once they were underway, she placed enough distance between them that he no longer felt her on his skin. Instead, wise in the way of walking in hostile land, she sought ground that allowed her to see as much as possible. Like the others, her gaze never left their surroundings. The presence of small birds meant no hawk or eagle was around. A deer eating a short distance away meant the creature didn't sense a cougar or wolf, or abuli. The deer's behavior also said it wasn't accustomed to humans and didn't perceive them as a threat.

The sun on his shoulders didn't feel quite as warm as it had yesterday, and it had been a little slower to arrive this morning, proof that summer was dying. Winter didn't bother him because he'd simply change to warmer clothes. And when the nights became endless, he'd spend them with the slave-whores—at least that's what he'd done in the past.

Now, watching Nuwaa who was part human and part wary, watchful animal, he wondered if he'd ever want to touch a slave-whore again.

Chapter Ten

Wonderful! Like coming back to life.

But even as the joy of doing what she'd been trained for swept over Nuwaa, she admitted she'd been far from dead while the ropes were on her.

Unwilling to explore what she'd experienced, she became part of her surroundings. The birds spoke of the simple task of feeding themselves while the breeze carried a taste of colder weather. The ground was dry, proof of how long it had been since it had rained, and like the other warriors, she was careful not to walk on leaves and other fallen things that might signal their presence. The sun was life to her shoulders and back, her spear as much a part of her as her breath.

Wolf Spirit, hear this warrior's song. I have been apart from you, but now I return to present myself to you for guidance.

Her spirit's response came in the form of the faintest feather-touch of alarm down her spine. At first she wondered if she was simply again reacting to Bor's presence, but she didn't fear him.

I fear nothing, she reminded herself. *Fear is not a warrior's way.*

But caution was.

She studied the others, but none seemed more alert than they'd been a moment ago. Yesterday they'd talked among themselves most of the day, but no one had spoken after starting this morning. She'd taken that as proof of their respect for the abuli and how little they knew about this place where their leader said they would spend the winter.

The feather-touch returned, and she stopped so she could concentrate on it. Out of the corner of her eye she spotted Bor studying her.

Listen, she mouthed.

She thought he might come closer or speak. Instead he too became motionless. One by one the others did the same, although the slave-whores first gathered in a close group.

What? Bor mouthed. She shook her head, then turned her attention back to her surroundings as the sense of alarm became stronger. As tense as she was, she also loved moments like this when every nerve felt on fire. She became sight, sound, smell.

Then she sensed an unexpected pressure on the earth caused by something living. The presence's rhythm became hers. She felt slow, steady movement coming toward them. They were in deep brush here, and although she strained to see, the vegetation kept its secrets. The birds fell silent.

Although she didn't dare shift her gaze, she knew Bor had increased his grip on his spear and had planted his weight evenly on both legs. She thought, briefly, about the power in those legs and the even greater power those legs sheltered.

The presence's pace increased. She felt the flow of energy from an unseen source. Straining, one with her world, she willed it to give up its secrets.

There. Behind her.

She turned slow and silent, the spear now gripped in both hands. Head up, weight on her toes, she waited.

The abuli exploded from the brush. As it charged her, it screamed high and loud and awful. She'd never seen an animal move that fast. The blur of its reddish body made it impossible for her to fully note its potential, but her mind recorded a massive head and powerful hindquarters.

She waited. Time all but stopped as she concentrated on the creature's speed. She became it, shared its muscles, its brain even. And in the half-heartbeat before it attacked, she leaped aside. At the same time she drove her spear into the beast. She'd aimed for its chest, but her own movement caused the spear to strike it in the shoulder.

Another scream, this one coated in rage, shook the air. She wanted to scream in reply. Instead, she jumped back and watched as its hindquarters flipped around so the abuli was again facing her. Its powerful lunge had taken it past her, and when it turned, the imbedded spear quivered. Perhaps pain had finally registered because the abuli stopped and bit at the spear. Although it managed to close its jaws around the shaft, it lacked the range of movement to pull it out.

Besides, its eyes left no doubt of its intention. It would kill the puny creature who'd dare to stand up to it. The next scream was lower, deep notes dragged up from beneath the ground. Trembling in anticipation, Nuwaa sent a single message to her legs. Once again she'd wait until the last moment, then jump aside unless the beast's speed outstripped hers.

It charged, feet clawing the earth, muscles starkly outlined beneath the thick fur. Nuwaa didn't have time for the attack to register. She simply reacted. Once more she managed to evade the beast, this time by springing backward. But as she did, she lost her footing and fell to her knees. Instead of springing back to her feet, she waited, learned, anticipated.

Turning. Screaming. Mouth open and dripping. Ears flat. Muscles speaking of terrible strength. She felt pinned down by the beast's yellow-eyed glare. *I will kill you*, its eyes said. *Tear you apart and feed on your still-beating heart.*

Then, suddenly, it sprang upward as if something had struck it a powerful blow. Another spear protruded from the red fur. This one was buried much deeper, an obscene decoration in its side. Blood poured from the second wound, and although the abuli clawed and bit at this new obscenity, it also lost the strength in its hindquarters. Slowly, almost gracefully, it collapsed onto its belly. Its head started to sag, jerked up for another scream, dropped to the ground.

"Nuwaa!"

Bor's voice. Bor's spear.

"Nuwaa! Are you all right?"

"Yes," she said as she watched the abuli's chest rise and fall. As it died, she prayed for its spirit to find peace. Then, not sure her legs would hold her, she stood. She'd taken a single step when Bor reached her and gathered her against him. She still felt numb. Her mind hadn't caught up with the actions of the past moments and instead of giving in to his embrace, she remained tense and alert.

The sound of running footsteps caught her attention and, still in Bor's arms, she turned to face the approaching Kebo warriors. Durc was in the lead. For the first time, his gaze didn't take in her body but remained fixed on her face.

"You are a warrior," he said, sounding out of breath. "I was certain the abuli would kill you but—"

"My spear did not end it," she pointed out. "Bor's did."

"But yours slowed it and was the first."

Durc was right. Besides, it felt good to hear his praise and see the looks of admiration from the other warriors. The Kebo might be the enemy, but for this moment they were equals.

"You showed no fear," Bor said. He kept his arm around her waist, not possessively but almost as if he thought she might disappear. "Your soul is brave."

"I prayed," she admitted. Looking down, she saw that the abuli had stopped breathing. *Go to your place of peace. Become one with your spirit.* "My spirit gave me strength and courage."

Durc chuckled and asked when she'd had time to think about asking her spirit for help. She didn't try to explain because surely he and the others knew that spirit-prayers were instinctive. She thought her legs might grow shaky, but they didn't. Perhaps Bor's touch kept her from thinking about what might have happened.

"I thank you," she told him. "Your spear killed him."

Still holding her, he kicked the inert form. "Yours would have, but it would have taken time."

Someone asked how she'd managed to respond so quickly, and she explained that she'd sensed the abuli's presence. She just hadn't known where it was until it sprang from the bushes.

"Now I fully understand," she admitted, "why the Kebo so respect the abuli. They are swift and silent killers."

Rasja pulled the spears out of the body and handed them to her and Bor. "She is right," he said, addressing everyone. "Abuli live to kill. If it had not attacked her, it would have been one of us. My reactions are slow. I would be dead."

Nuwaa couldn't say whether the older warrior was right. She was just grateful that, so far, no one had suggested that if a woman hadn't been among the Kebo warriors, maybe the abuli wouldn't have attacked. She didn't bother to point out that what she'd done served as proof that she was hardly a mere captive.

Heat beneath where Bor's fingers rested brought her attention back to him and made her wonder why he'd said so little. He brought the bloody spear point to his nostrils and inhaled, then let her do the same. Next he held the spear over his head.

"One abuli will never again threaten the Kebo," he said. "But when will we know if all of them have been killed? Will we be able to hunt them down or must we wait until they attack?"

Nodding heads indicated that everyone agreed.

"I will take the head and pelt back to Liege-lord Haddard, lay it at his feet, and ask if coming here is worth the risk."

More heads nodded, but no one spoke. She couldn't imagine a Sakar questioning one of Liege-lord Radislay's decisions and wondered how the Kebo leader would respond. Even if the question came from his war-liege, surely it would anger him.

The slave-whores had ventured close and were staring, not at the abuli but at her and Bor. Sensing their tension, she tried to find its source. True, they had ample reason to be apprehensive about the possibility of more abuli being nearby, but maybe the thought of conflict between the two most powerful men in the clan was making them nervous.

"You know what an abuli is capable of," she ventured. "If you tell your liege-lord that this area is unsafe and refuse to bring the Kebo here, will he listen?"

"Refuse?" Bor all but glared down at her. "You want me to turn my back on my liege-lord?"

"No," she quickly amended. "But what if you and Haddard are not of the same mind? Do you always give way before him because of who he is?"

Grunts from a number of the men warned her that she'd gone too far with her question. Bor's expression turned angry. "What takes place between my liege-lord and me is not your concern, Captive!"

You cannot easily answer me, can you? she thought. *You are a warrior, not your liege-lord's slave.*

Even as she busied herself by wiping blood off her spear, she wondered whether her life might eventually depend on his reaction to her question.

* * * * *

Bor chose a spot sheltered from the wind by a rocky outcropping where the warriors would spend their final night away from the rest of the clan. He'd seldom given thought to where the slave-whores would stay when they weren't being used, but this time he made sure their separate area afforded shelter too. Perhaps most important, he spotted a small, secluded flat space for him and Nuwaa some distance from the others.

He hadn't spoken to her since the abuli killing. Although he'd spent much of the rest of the day thinking about what she'd said, he still wasn't sure what he'd say to her. He'd taken care not to walk near her and had suspected she felt the same way because she'd stayed close to the rest of the men, a slender, proud figure existing somewhere between warrior and prisoner.

He'd never met anyone like her and never suspected such women existed. He wanted to drink endlessly of her and house his cock in her cave over and over again, to place his hands on her and feel her warmth, her life. As summers faded, the women collected overripe berries and let them ferment. When their smell indicated they were ready, the warriors ate the berries and drank the juices and lost contact with their minds. With his belly and brain full, he laughed and sang and felt like a child again. Worn-out slave-whores became young in his mind, and he fucked until he couldn't any more. He felt like that whenever he looked at Nuwaa, which was why he'd avoided her today. Now, however, it was time to take her to his bed.

Not bothering to acknowledge his fellow warriors, he walked over to where she sat, looking into the fire, and grabbed her arm. He sensed her hesitancy. However, although he thought he might have to force her to obey, she got to her feet and silently followed him. He'd arranged for several warriors to take turns guarding the others during the night so gave only passing thought to other abuli.

"We will not speak today of what you said about what exists between me and my liege-lord," he ordered. "It was not your place. It will not happen again."

"You have never asked yourself the question?"

A heartbeat away from slapping her, he instead gripped her shoulders. "Do not forget what you are, my captive. I hold your life in my hands."

He expected her to point out that she could have escaped today, but she didn't. Instead, he felt her tremble.

"You fear me?" he asked.

"No."

No. How complex things were between them. Wondering if he'd correctly sensed her emotion, he slid a hand down her shoulder while reaching under her shirt with the other so he could close it over her breast. Her trembling increased, and she tried to take hold of his cock. Instead, her fingers closed over his loincloth.

"Do not touch me," he warned. "I have not given you permission."

Although he felt her spine straighten, her arms dropped to her sides. She continued to look up at him, her features only faintly outlined by the moon. Wondering at her reaction and thoughts, he embraced his superiority. In his mind, she again became his captive, but this time he knew how he'd react to her body and how fragile was his self-control. He'd have to both keep a grip on his emotions and take control of hers.

"You displeased me today," he said and positioned her hands behind her. "I will not punish you because you may have saved the lives of Kebo warriors, but you do not understand who and what you have become. Say it. You are my captive."

Her response was a sharp intake of breath. He pressed her hands against her buttocks. "Say it."

"I am your captive."

Even her voice trembled now, causing him to feel stronger than he had a moment ago. He loved his sense of power, needed this because otherwise she'd weaken him.

"I bow before your courage," he continued as he gripped both slender wrists in one hand and moved to her side. "Your actions today show that you were a worthy warrior, but you no longer are." He ran his free hand under her skirt and pressed against her belly. "You are again my possession."

Instead of trying to break free, she nodded. He sensed her legs were weakening and took advantage by sliding his hand between her legs. She didn't try to resist but opened herself slightly. His fingers immediately became wet. His cock throbbed.

"What are you going to do with me?" she whispered.

"You do not know?" His forefinger found and penetrated her opening.

"Not now. Tomorrow."

In truth he wished tomorrow would never come. "Present you to my liege-lord," he said because there'd never been any doubt of that.

"I thought perhaps because of what happened between us that you would keep me for yourself."

I want! How I want!

"My liege-lord has long wanted a Sakar woman-warrior. I will deliver that captive to him."

Her sigh struck him as being somewhere between relief and regret, but he could barely concentrate because her cunt muscles were closing and relaxing around his finger. Although he kept his eyes open, his vision turned red. His head pounded in time with his heartbeat, and he thought of nothing except replacing his finger with his cock.

But if he didn't fuck her in the way of a warrior instead of a man, he risked losing himself in her.

Determined not to let that happen, he pushed her so she stumbled back and down, landing on her ass. She'd just started to get onto her knees when he dropped beside her and roughly tore off her top. "Do not move," he warned. "Remember what you are and that I own you."

She made fists of her fingers, and he guessed she was clenching her teeth. Although her breathing continued to be that of a sexually aroused woman, he sensed her battle with self-control.

It didn't matter. This, his last night with her, meant everything. He was a warrior, a warrior!

Nuwaa didn't resist when Bor pushed her onto her back and bent her legs.

Be what he thinks you are, she struggled to remind herself. *Be a captive who has become a slave to her body and her master's cock. You are nothing else, nothing!*

For tonight, she amended before forcing the thought to the back of her mind.

When he stretched her arms over her head, she left them there even though she wasn't bound. He pushed her skirt up around her waist and removed his loincloth before leaning down over her and taking a nipple in his mouth.

She shouldn't have come here with him! She should have—what? Although she imagined herself refusing his earlier order or fighting him, the results would have been the same because his strength outstripped hers.

Besides, despite the danger, she needed this.

Whimpering low in her throat, she grabbed handfuls of grass and held on. Her head rocked from side to side. He'd trapped her pussy under his body, leaving it crying to be touched.

She needed this! Needed to be taken.

Embracing the sensation of having given up ownership of her body, she waited for him to do what he wanted with it. It did no good to even think of resistance because he must know how much she wanted to be fucked, so she simply continued to whimper and try to lift her spine off the ground so he might take more of her breast into his mouth. After a few moments, he stopped, simply holding her nipple, and began bathing it with his saliva. He licked and sucked, deposited and drank. She ground her buttocks into the earth and pulled on the grass. When he turned his attention to her other breast, she sighed and shifted to bring it within easy reach. He took his time wetting this breast, then briefly warmed the other. Fluid dribbled from her sex. Even if he couldn't see, he must know how she was reacting.

Just as she was wondering if she could come from his manipulation of her breasts, he rocked back and gripped her hips.

"Lift your legs," he ordered. "Pull your thighs against your belly."

Too lost for anything except obedience, she did as he said. She had to grip her ankles to keep them in place, which left her looking at what she could see of her legs.

"Keep them there. No matter what I do, you are not to let your legs down until I give you permission.

Permission? He was testing her, and tonight she lacked the will to do anything except comply. He touched something against her pussy, and although she briefly tensed, she soon relaxed. The tip of his cock felt right brushing her labia. His penis moved easily, stroking the length of her cunt. Not being able to move or see still left her feeling vulnerable, but if she didn't willing follow his order, he'd force her.

Would she ever want that?

She couldn't answer, couldn't do anything except experience.

The strokes shortened and became more focused around her opening. She thought she might come just waiting for him to push into her, and yet she loved the waiting, the anticipation.

Then he drove into her. When he pushed, she felt herself slide slightly. Her body seemed to wedge itself against the fur under her and she remained in place, a receptacle for him. His cock engulfed her and when he closed his fingers over her thighs, she realized he'd stolen all movement from her. For as long as he wanted, she would remain trapped between him and the ground, unable to participate in the invasion of flesh against flesh.

She imagined him on his knees, pelvis and thighs and buttocks all working together so he could endlessly pummel her. His cock scraped, slid, glided over the length of her cave. She felt herself begin to seep into him and lose substance and form. Only her pussy existed, a pussy whose urgent muscle contractions were beyond her ability to control.

Her climax was just there, barely out of reach when he shifted his grip so his hands covered her hipbones.

"Let go of your legs," he hissed. "Hands over your head again."

As she struggled to obey the complex order, her legs fell forward so they dangled over his back but were held high by his arms and shoulders. He'd managed to immobilize her even more than she'd been before. Not content with this increased control, he lifted her buttocks off the ground, expertly positioning her so her cunt was in alignment with his cock. Throughout the change, he'd remained tight in her.

Now he began thrusting again, shaking her, driving into her, pounding her with his weapon.

Used.

The word died under the climax that clawed over her. She felt nothing except her hot, clenching muscles and knew nothing except wave after wave. She'd just begun to sense her climax releasing its grip on her when he came. Grunting long and low, he shoved into her and held there. His cock expanded, shuddered. Cum filled her.

When, finally, he relaxed, he lowered her to the ground again. By the way his hands lingered on her belly and thighs, she wondered if he'd hold her through the night. But although he remained beside her for several moments, he abruptly pushed her away, and turned his back to her. By his breathing, she knew he wasn't falling asleep.

"Bor," she whispered. "What—"

"Silence!"

"I cannot. Tomorrow—"

"Tomorrow I will do my duty," he muttered. Then he pushed himself to his feet and walked out into the night.

Chapter Eleven

Nuwaa hadn't known what to expect so wasn't surprised by the cluster of *mogans* that made a rough circle in a treeless area. She suspected the open space had been chosen because it made it harder for an enemy to approach undetected. Although she couldn't see the source of water, she guessed a creek or lake was responsible for the lush vegetation a short distance away.

The Sakar kept pigs in a wood and rope enclosure so they'd have ready access to meat provided by the fat-bodied creatures, but from what she could tell, the Kebo had made no attempt to control the movements of any of the area's wildlife. She wondered at a clan that relied solely on what hunters could provide and understood even better than she had before why her liege-lord was determined to do everything he could to make sure the Kebo didn't try to take what belonged to the Sakar.

The Kebo were meat-eaters, attackers who took whatever they could. She must never forget that they thought of the Sakar as their prey.

When she'd gotten up this morning, Bor had ordered her to place her hands in front of her so he could tie them. Then he'd placed a noose around her neck and used that to lead her. Someone else now carried her spear, and she was naked from the waist up. His message was clear. She was once again a captive, a prisoner he was determined to deliver to his liege-lord.

Children had run out to greet them before they reached the village, obviously delighted to see the warriors, marginally curious about her, and fascinated by the fresh head and pelt Bor carried. From what she could tell, none had seen an abuli and were full of questions about who had killed it and how. Instead of trying to answer the barrage of questions, he made it clear that he intended to tell the story once when everyone in the clan had gathered around.

As soon as they reached the village itself, people seemed to materialize from everywhere. She was struck by the number of women carrying babies. By the way the woman acted, she perceived them as having a kinship of sorts. They were all comfortable in each other's presence and seemed willing to care for whatever toddler came near. They also made no effort to hide their delight at seeing certain warriors and there were open displays of affection. Among her people, such regard among couples was frowned upon because Liege-lord Radislay insisted that the men were first and foremost warriors. Needs of the flesh were satisfied in private. Also, women of childbearing years seldom mingled with warriors in public because a mother was considered sacred.

Confused by the differences between the two clans, she was slow to realize Bor was leading her to the center pit. Although no fire was burning during the heat of the day, the area also obviously served as the clan's general meeting place. Several seats made of wood and leather had been positioned so that those sitting in them appeared taller than those who perched on uncomfortable-looking logs.

A large wrinkled man with a great mane of white hair sat in the most prominent chair. His face and what she could see of his arms and legs had been painted with a number of colorful symbols making it nearly impossible to distinguish his features. A lion pelt was draped over his shoulders, and his loincloth was decorated with numerous colorful bird feathers. He carried a long, slim spear with a tip made of shinning black stone. The spear would make a poor weapon, but the carvings along its length were elaborate, obviously the work of a skilled craftsman.

Bor walked up to the large man and deposited the abuli head at his feet. Then he abruptly yanked down on her neck rope. Caught unaware, she fell to her knees. Bor immediately stepped on the rope so her head was nearly on the ground. Unable to see, she stared at the earth.

"She is young," the man she knew was Liege-lord Haddard said. "I expected her to be older."

"She is a warrior," Bor said without emotion.

"I say she is nothing more than a captive."

"After what she did, I cannot call her that."

Trying to see what was going on was useless which left her with no option except to support the upper part of her body as best she could with her bound hands. She hated what Bor was doing to her, and yet had she expected anything different? Their time together had been a dream while this was reality.

Footsteps and excited voices told her that a large number of people, perhaps the entire village, were joining those already at the center firepit. People continued to ask Bor and the other warriors about her and the dead abuli, but perhaps he'd answered with his eyes, because before long they fell silent.

The women she'd spotted had all been dressed much more elaborately than the men, who for the most part hadn't bothered with anything except loincloths. Having her ass barely covered while her naked breasts brushed the ground served as unmistakable reminder of her position here. The Kebo considered their captives as less than human—just as her own people did.

Once everyone had settled down, Bor began with the attack by the Sakar. Hearing the tale brought back painful memories of seeing Tabathi die, and she fought tears. Several people muttered that she deserved the harshest punishment when Bor said she was responsible for his wound.

"Silence," a man ordered. From the direction of the voice, she had no doubt it was Haddard. "I will decide her fate."

Because she'd expected nothing different and because she needed to be alone with him if she stood a chance of completing her mission, she felt a measure of relief at his words.

She also had no doubt of her ultimate fate.

Bor had started speaking again, and she lost herself, not so much in his words as the sound of his voice. The tone made her feel as if a feather was being brushed over her breasts, belly, buttocks, and cunt.

"The captive struck the first blow against the abuli," Bor said. "She did not try to run from its attack but immediately threw her spear. The abuli died with her weapon buried in it."

"Her weapon?" Liege-lord Haddard questioned. "Why was she armed?"

For too long no one spoke. She couldn't imagine what Bor was thinking or how he'd answer his liege-lord.

"Because I saw into her heart and found a warrior, not a captive."

Liege-lord Haddard didn't ask for an explanation, and after a moment, Bor continued speaking. Her back ached. She, who had maybe saved lives defending Kebo warriors against an abuli, felt humiliated. Bor could have refused to treat her as his liege-lord had commanded. But wasn't she willing to sacrifice her own life in order to obey the man she considered her god? How could she expect anything different from Bor?

"Prepare for a feast," Liege-lord Haddard announced when Bor had finished. "We celebrate."

Enthusiastic stomping of countless feet left no doubt of everyone's reaction. The gathering started breaking up, but she remained held in place.

"Take her inside," Liege-lord Haddard commanded. "Tie her as a captive is tied."

* * * * *

This Kebo *mogan* was the largest such structure she'd ever seen. Constructed of tightly woven branches with a leaf roof supported by several poles, it easily had enough room for all the warriors who'd been with Bor, but right now she and Bor were the only ones in it. As her eyes adjusted to the dim lighting, she noted it contained several wooden carvings depicting various animals and birds. In addition, someone had painted elaborate figures on tightly stretched hides. These figures were of creatures which appeared to be half-animal and half-human. Most appeared to have either the sun or moon in the background. With a shudder she realized these must be Kebo gods. Most prominent was a man figure with a massive bear head. To her shock, Bor dropped to his knees before that figure and touched his head to the ground much in the way he'd forced her to kneel.

He stayed there for a while, muttering what she believed was a prayer while still holding onto her neck rope. She thought he might force her to grovel before the image, but he didn't.

Finally he stood and, without speaking to her, transferred the neck rope to her wrists and tied that to the center pole, forcing her to lift her hands over her head. He turned as if to leave.

"What is going to happen?" she demanded. "What is he going to do to me?"

"He is Haddard, offspring of the god of gods." He indicated the bear-man figure. "In this place he becomes a god himself."

The too-dark enclosure was indeed impressive. If she'd been raised a Kebo, she too would have felt awed surrounded by the gods. Although she hadn't grown up worshipping these spirits, she felt small and weak before their power. Even Bor seemed diminished.

"You do not care?" she ventured. "If he places a knife at my throat you will not try to stop him."

"You no longer belong to me."

I never did.

"Go then," she hissed.

He stared.

"Go! I wash you out of me." She indicated the space between her legs.

"Do you?" He closed the distance between them, reached under her skirt, and planted his hand over her opening.

She should ask herself why he was doing this, should decide whether she wanted him here when Haddard arrived. But his possessive hand brought back so many memories. In her mind she heard herself scream out a climax. In the world she lived in, she moaned as need far stronger than the fear she'd been denying, claimed her.

Still holding on to her, Bor covered a breast and began touching her in a manner that was somewhere between pain and pleasure.

"Why?" she demanded as she unsuccessfully tried to free herself. "Why are you doing this?"

"You are a cunt, a slave-whore, nothing to a warrior."

Even as his grip grew more insistent, she believed she understood. If he could get her to say she hated him then the connection between them would be broken. When he looked back over their time together, he'd tell himself he'd taken what had been his as the victor. She'd simply been his possession, his slave-whore and cunt.

"May coyotes feed on your entrails," she hissed. "Hear my prayers, gods of the Sakar. Cut this animal open and leave his carcass for the buzzards."

"Sakar gods cannot hear you here," he growled rather than spoke. "Only Kebo spirits know of this place." Although he'd already been gripping her breast so tight that tears had sprung to her eyes, he increased the pressure. Unable to help herself, she sobbed.

Perhaps the sound reached him in some private place because his hold relaxed. He continued to lay claim to her pussy, but his touch was no longer that of a conqueror. Instead, he dipped two fingers into her and pressed as if taking some of her wet heat for himself. She needed to remember the punishment! Needed to hate and curse!

But she couldn't because she now stood trapped and helpless, soft flesh quivering beneath his expert assault and his knowledge of her. Her head rolled forward. She needed to focus on her surroundings so she could understand what gods ruled the Kebo, but how could she when he was turning her into a wolf-bitch. She danced on his fingers and made no move to wrestle back freedom of her breast. And she moaned over and over again.

"How well-trained."

Bor stiffened but didn't turn from her. He looked down at her, but she didn't know what he was thinking and couldn't muster the self-awareness to see if he had an erection.

"I applaud you," Liege-lord Haddard said as he came closer. "Only a few nights with the captive and she has become a cunt for you."

If Bor was angry, he gave no indication.

"You were testing her for me?" Haddard asked. "Making sure she is ready for her master's touch?"

Bor didn't move, didn't speak. And he still claimed her.

"What made you think I wanted to fuck her?" Haddard asked. Something about his tone set off a shiver in her. Had she heard the voice before? "Perhaps I only wanted her brought back so I could watch an enemy bleed to death." Coming to stand next to Bor, he started caressing her throat. Before she could gather her thoughts around the touch, the liege-lord of the Kebo claimed her other breast. "Go," he ordered Bor. "You have turned her over to me. Your responsibility has ended."

Even before Bor released her and stepped back, she'd sensed his inner battle. Unquestioning loyalty to one's liege-lord was essential for a warrior. Bor had certainly spent season upon season putting his leader's safety and wishes before his own. He'd die for this god-man just as she was willing to die for her liege-lord.

Bor now stood slightly behind Haddard, and although she didn't dare take her eyes off the man who dictated whether she would live or die, she made no attempt to shake off Bor's impact on her senses. Hunger continued to assault her, and it took self-control to remain still. She, who valued freedom above all else, had been content to stand helpless before one man. She, who had the soul of a warrior, would have begged to be fucked if they'd been alone.

"Go," Haddard repeated. "I will want you back in here in a while but first the captive and I will speak."

Bor shouldn't have stood there as long as he did because an obedient warrior would immediately heed his liege-lord's commands. But only after a long, heavy silence did he drop to his knees and lower his head to the ground in front of the bear-man carving before pushing aside the hide door and walking out.

Haddard squeezed her breast and throat then stepped back. For the first time she looked, truly looked at him. Despite the face decorations and poor lighting, she finally noted his features. A shudder seized her.

"You know," Haddard said softly.

* * * * *

"I will not kill you. Yet."

Haddard grabbed her skirt and pulled it down, leaving it around her ankles. Because he'd gagged her, she couldn't have responded even if she'd wanted to.

"If I did, my war-liege might forget that I am his god." He selected a long, thin branch from the wood near the firepit. "But I do not keep you alive because I fear his wrath."

Drawing back his hand, he struck a blow on her belly with the slender branch. Although it stung, the pain wasn't enough to distract her from what she needed to concentrate on. These moments with Haddard were everything. Whatever she learned, she would take back to her people if she ever could.

"You will tell me certain things." He stopped speaking to whip her belly several more times. "I know how the man you call Liege-lord Radislay trains and prepares his warriors. You would allow me to cut out your tongue before you would tell me of the Sakar's weaknesses. But that will not be necessary because by the time I am done with you, you will do whatever I demand of you."

He struck her again and again, each blow leaving welts but not breaking her skin. When she turned away from him, he lashed her back and buttocks. Desperate to escape what felt like countless bee stings, she twisted one way and then the other. She bit down on the length of leather he'd forced into her mouth, but although she couldn't control her ragged breathing, she refused to cry out.

"He hates me, does he not?" Although Haddard now sounded slightly out of breath, he hit her over and over again as a drummer strikes his drum. "Your liege-lord wants me dead."

Unwilling to lie, she let her eyes speak for her. Haddard stopped beating her and rocked back on his heels. Sadness so deep she couldn't fathom its depths, flashed across his features.

"I listened to my war-liege's tale of how he came to capture you." He held up the switch, seemingly content knowing she couldn't take her eyes off it. "Only one Sakar warrior was caught—you. The others escaped."

Bor rendered me unconscious.

"You could have run," he said, as if reading her mind. Rocking forward, he rested the branch between her breasts. "A woman with full breasts and hips made for housing a man's cock. Tell me, Captive. You were not simply unworthy of fighting the Kebo. You wanted to be caught."

She struggled to hide her reaction, but he grabbed a nipple and roughly twisted it. "This!" He shook her breast. "This your Sakar leader believes will make a Kebo forget who is his enemy. How carefully he chose you. And my war-liege fell under your spell."

Pain spread through her, the sensation a world away from what she'd experienced with Bor. She wanted to tell this man that she knew all too well that Bor was no simple creature caring about nothing except fucking, but as long as he held her nipple like that, she couldn't think. She'd known she might be tortured but this, this—

"Rest a moment," Haddard said with unexpected tenderness. After yet another squeeze, he released her breast. Blood rushed into her nipple. "We have only begun," he said with his face so close to hers that she could feel the heat of his breath. "By the time I am done with you, I will know everything."

Her struggles had caused the ropes to rub against her wrists. In an effort to decrease the discomfort, she stood on tiptoe. Chuckling, he reached between her legs. Instinct claimed her, and she lashed out with her foot, striking his thigh a glancing blow.

"You fight. Good."

Raging against her helplessness, she could only watch as he stepped to the door and walked out.

* * * * *

"How many times did you fuck her?"

Bor had been sitting with his fellow warriors as they waited for the pungent-smelling meat to finish cooking. The others were only too happy to recall their adventures of the past few days for the curious clustered around, but he'd heard little of what was being said. Instead, his mind had been in the sacred *mogan* as he wondered what was taking place between his liege-lord and the captive. When he'd spotted Haddard leaving it, it had taken all his self-control not to jump up and hurry inside. Because he hadn't, he had no choice but to answer his liege-lord as best he could with everyone listening.

"I do not know," he admitted. Her hands, breasts, and the space between her legs swirled together in his mind.

"Did you rape her?"

All conversation stopped. "No."

"Because she was in heat?" Haddard demanded. "Because you are such a mighty warrior that she turned into a cunt?"

"I do not know what drove her."

"Do you care?"

Do you care? Because he'd never admit how much he needed to know the truth, he remained silent.

"Come with me," Haddard ordered. "She waits."

* * * * *

No matter how many times he'd been in the sacred *mogan*, Bor never ceased to feel a sense of awe. Before the gods had sent Liege-lord Haddard to them, the Kebo had been a loosely connected band of travelers barely able to protect themselves against invaders. The men had relied on spirit-gods, but no one had suspected how powerful those gods were and how promising allegiance to them would enrich their lives. Now, although the Kebo still lived primarily as nomads, they put down temporary roots as the seasons changed. Instead of seeking shelter in the wilderness, they built *mogans*. Their god-given liege-lord had taught men how to be true warriors and had shown the women that being mothers meant they were respected above all others. Babies were protected and loved, children slowly shown the journey to productive adulthood. No longer dependent on an individual hunter's generosity in sharing his kill, every piece of meat belonged to the clan. Lean bellies filled out under his guidance, and women's breasts grew heavy with the milk their babies needed to flourish. The Kebo were no longer prey but predators.

None of those things would have happened without the offspring of Lifelight, god of gods.

Surrounded by this proof of his leader's power and responsibility, he dropped to his knees and prayed before standing. Nuwaa stood where he'd left her, arms still bound over her head. Although she was now naked, he paid little attention to that. Even in the faint light he could tell she'd been whipped and wore a gag. Fighting the urge to tend to her, he waited for Haddard to join him.

"Tell me, War-liege, what are you thinking?"

"Why is she silent? I thought you wanted her to tell you certain things."

"I did." Liege-lord Haddard picked up something and handed it to him. Bor had no doubt this was the switch he'd used on her. "But before I allow her to speak, she must learn of my power."

And you didn't want me hearing if she cried out. Wondering if his leader might command him to whip her, he fought the urge to break the switch in small pieces.

"Look at her," Liege-lord Haddard ordered. "She is not bleeding."

But close, so close.

"She is a warrior." Haddard's voice was full of admiration. "I thought she might be less, a simple female allowed to call herself a warrior because she pleases the creature she and the other Sakar follow, but she is more."

"She stood strong and proud before the abuli," Bor pointed out. "Not once has she begged or cried."

"And when the two of you fuck, does she come?"

Not sure where the conversation was going, he nodded. Nuwaa's arms weren't stretched so tight that they should cause her great pain, but he still hated seeing her like this, hated not knowing what his liege-lord intended to do with her.

"A beating teaches a captive that she no longer has ownership of her body," Haddard said. "But if she speaks it is only because she will do whatever she can to stop the pain. It does not mean her words are the truth."

"What do you want her to say?"

Haddard was silent for so long that Bor tore his gaze off Nuwaa who stared at him as if she wanted him dead.

"Why she was sent here. And what her liege-lord told her about the Kebo, about me."

He'd never heard that tone from his lord before. The words made him think of a grieving child. "Ask her," he said.

Haddard grunted. "I will, but not until she has no more defenses and only the truth remains."

Feeling sick, he waited for the order to start beating her, but hadn't Haddard just said that pain didn't always give birth to the truth?

"You became more than her captor," Haddard continued. "That is why she was armed when the abuli attacked, because you saw her as an equal."

Where was this heading? Was his liege-lord going to tell him he'd failed as war-liege of the Kebo?

Moving with a speed he didn't often see from his liege-lord, Haddard stepped behind Nuwaa, gripped an ass cheek in his powerful fingers, and rammed the side of his other hand against her cunt. She growled and struggled to free herself.

"Here is the truth," Liege-lord Haddard declared. "Together you and I will pull it out of her."

Chapter Twelve

Although she fought the two men, they easily retied Nuwaa in the position Liege-lord Haddard ordered. She now sat with her weight on her buttocks, her back arched and her shoulders and head resting on a wall. Her arms were back over her head. What she truly hated was that they'd forced her legs far apart. They were held in place with ropes around her ankles, and more ropes were around her knees, keeping them somewhat bent and off the ground. The gag remained in place. Air whispered over her exposed cunt.

"It is said that a man thinks with his cock," Haddard announced as he stood between her legs and stared down at her. "The same is true of a woman. Once her cunt has come to life, it rules her."

Despite the need to keep her attention on Haddard, she risked a look in Bor's direction, but he'd stepped back, placing his features in shadow. His arms were at his side, his stance alert.

"Only savages make no use of their captives," Haddard went on, making her wonder if his intention was to reassure Bor. What did she care! Bor had participated in doing this to her! "Those who understand what matters most to a human know how to use that weakness to their advantage."

Haddard extended his foot. She had no doubt he was moving slowly so she'd be forced to anticipate. When his toes touched her sex, she tried to jerk free. "Listen to me,

Captive," he said as he wiggled his toes against her opening. "By the time I am done with you, you will tell me everything. If I removed your gag now, I would hear the truth of a thinking mind." His big toe found her opening and slid in. "I need that mind silent."

"What do you want from her?" Bor demanded.

"Patience, War-liege. You will soon understand, but first I require your help in turning her into a cunt, an animal in heat."

She hadn't needed to hear the words to know what this monster had in mind. Why hadn't her liege-lord warned her this might happen! Why had he sent her, a woman, on this mission? A tremor hit her as she realized that Radislay must have suspected this outcome. He'd decided to sacrifice her but why?

Why!

Haddard removed his foot from her core, but she knew better than to believe he'd granted her a reprieve.

"Tell me something." He was addressing Bor. "If I ordered you to cause her pain, would you?"

"No."

"Ah, the truth. Is it because your loyalty lies now with her and not me?"

"No."

"Which is it, Bor?" Haddard demanded. "Do I, your god and leader come first in your heart or has the captive stolen it?"

Bor's silence told her he was in too much conflict to respond.

"I test you today, Bor," Haddard continued. "Listen to me. Listen and believe. This female warrior is only the beginning. She was sent here to learn of our weaknesses. Her mission was to take her knowledge back to the man she calls Liege-lord Radislay. At least she believed that was her only mission. But her leader looked at her and knew she had a greater purpose. He knew that she, with her woman's body, had the power to reach past a man's defenses and could uncover weaknesses even that man did not suspect."

Haddard walked over to a pelt with several items on it and picked up the severed tail from a grass-eating dasha. Stroking the long, thick hairs, he repositioned himself between her legs. "This is your lesson, Captive. A man's weakness is also a woman's." He drew the tail over her pussy, each soft but strong hair touched nerves she'd been struggling to deny. She pressed her ass against the ground. Another stroke followed the first. Then another came so fast she had no time to shake off the sensual impact of the one that had come before. Again and again the fibers caressed her lips and clit. Although she knew it would do no good, she continued to try to move out of reach.

"No pain and yet agony," Haddard said as she felt her juices bubble to the surface. "Needing but not receiving release."

Mewling behind the gag, she struggled to remain still. These touches weren't enough! She needed more than sensation on the outside. Her core throbbed, hunger growing.

"You hate me, do you not, Captive? You want nothing more than my death. But you are unarmed and helpless to stop me."

Despite the red haze her world had become, she noted that Bor was coming closer. He now stood just behind his liege-lord but positioned so he had a clear view of her crudely exposed sex. The strokes continued, sometimes long and soft, sometimes short and jerky. Her temples pulsed, but even as the sensation over her pussy expanded and grew deeper, she knew she could survive this. Animal hairs could only touch so many nerves, awaken so many needs.

"Think of her as a hide," Haddard was saying. "When first handled, flesh left in the sun to dry is tough and barely workable. But as a woman continues to pound it, it becomes pliable. In the end, it is soft. It bends into whatever shape the woman desires. It does not break but is pliable like spring grass. Turn her into spring grass, my war-liege."

She thought he'd turn the tail over to Bor. Instead, Haddard directed him to return to the pelt for something he called the trainer. The word was enough to send chills through her. When she saw what Bor now held, she shuddered. A thick wad of hide in the shape of a penis had been attached to a short pole.

"When a female captive is being trained as a slave-whore, she spends much time with this in her," Haddard told her. "At first she fights and begs to be spared, but in time she will do anything to dance on it."

The slave-whore who'd led her that one day had mentioned techniques the men used to break the slave's spirit. Now she understood what had only been alluded to. Struggling not to whimper, she tensed and waited.

"I could make this my task," Haddard said to Bor. "In truth, I would love to be in charge of her *training*, but it will have more impact if you, who are trained in such things, administer the lessons."

"And then?"

"Ah, spoken like a man who has handed his cock to a woman. Listen to me, War-liege. She will live. For now you do not need to know anything more. Now, are you ready to obey your god?"

"Live?"

"I have spoken. Lifelight hears my words."

"So have I." Bor continued to stand motionless, looking into her eyes, his expression unfathomable. "For her to be alive is not enough. She must not bleed or be rendered unconscious."

For a moment she sensed a power struggle between the two men, but much as she wanted Bor to win, she needed to learn a great deal about Liege-lord Haddard. If he didn't stay near her, she might not ever fully comprehend.

"If you use this—" Haddard indicated the *trainer*, "—as I know you are capable, she will not want you to stop." When Bor didn't respond, Haddard addressed her. "Listen to me, Captive. Our war-liege is skilled in more than fighting and hunting. He understands that sometimes pulling secrets out of our enemies means the difference between success and failure. You will try to fight. But in the end, we will win."

Win what?

"Begin," Haddard said.

Despite the tremendous effort she put into it, she couldn't stop from trying to stay out of Bor's reach as he knelt between her legs and placed his hand on her labia.

"Feel his power," Haddard said. "Become one with him and what he does."

At first Bor did nothing more than press against her, the heel of his hand grinding against her lips while his fingers played with her mons. After a few moments, he switched direction so his palm covered her dark hairs and one finger after another by turn dipped into her. She felt him at her entrance, the promise of deep penetration there but unrealized. At the same time, he distracted her by running the *trainer* over her breasts. Bit by bit she became one with the object that glided lightly over her flesh.

He was running the tip from her throat down to between her breasts and up again when she realized he'd begun kneading her pussy. Although she felt splintered, she struggled to keep the two sensations separate. The heat that had been simmering up inside her heated and nothing she did or thought extinguished it.

"How can a woman hate this?" Haddard asked. "She might be uncomfortable tied like this and perhaps she is terrified because she does not know what is going to happen, but the movements, the sensations are irresistible."

Two—or was it three—fingers housed themselves in her opening. Bor straightened and relaxed them, straightened and relaxed. Her head grew heavy, and she let it fall back.

"A woman cannot say no to this," Haddard continued. "Her spirit rebels, yes, but her body does not hear the warning. She needs what is offered and promised. What may or may not come."

His words swirled in her mind. Perhaps he was trying to warn her, but about what?

"Show me," Haddard said.

Bor had deserted her opening, leaving her empty! She lifted her head in time to see him extending his glistening fingers in Haddard's direction.

"Good, good." Haddard sounded, not like a warrior applauding another's skill, but a man whose cock has begun speaking its own language.

Questions about whether he might force himself on her made her slow to realize Bor was aiming the *trainer* at her pussy. Not breathing, she studied the muscles and tendons in his forearm. Because of the way she'd been positioned, she couldn't see herself between her legs. She felt something touch the entrance to her opening and continued holding her breath.

"Feed her," Haddard said. "Only a little so she will know what hunger feels like."

The *trainer* parted her lips but stopped, promise and threat waiting and ready. Against all sanity, she tried to suck it into her.

"Ah, good, good."

Haddard was leaning over so he could see around Bor's forearm. Although she might have been able to bring the men's features into focus, she hid behind the veil clouding her world.

"So hungry, Captive. Eager for the promise to be fulfilled. But you have not earned it."

What? Before she could pull her thoughts together, Bor drew the *trainer* out of her. She sobbed at the loss and tried to thrust her pelvis at him. Even as she did, she cursed her weakness.

I hate you and what you are doing to me!

Not knowing whether she was directing her rage at one or both men, she willed her muscles to relax. She'd barely settled back when the *trainer* found her again. This time it dipped a little deeper and stayed housed in her a little longer.

It felt like a cock, and yet it lacked the warmth of life. Still, her pussy would have swallowed it if it could.

Again, again, and again the *trainer* fucked her. Sometimes it slipped in so deep she knew she couldn't take any more. Other times Bor barely touched her with it. She ached for hard, fast movement duplicating a man's thrusts, but he never gave her that. Instead, the untiring manmade cock worked her until she felt exhausted. At the same time, her hunger remained an unrelenting, gnawing need that circled throughout her and became everything.

If only she could climax! But Bor obviously knew more about her body than she did because he managed to keep her at the edge and never let her tumble. Never granted her release.

"This is dancing, Captive," she dimly heard Haddard say. "Dancing to a beat you hate because you cannot escape it. Think on this. If I so command, it will go on until you scream and beg. But your cries will change nothing. I hold you in my embrace, I, because Bor does as I command."

All the time he was speaking, Bor continued his relentless assault on her nerves and sanity. Did he want to be doing this? Did he even ask himself the question? Caught in the midst of what he was capable of doing to her senses, she couldn't say whether she hated him or would grovel at his feet if possible.

"Do you want to rest, Captive?"

Because she had no doubt that she wouldn't be granted a climax and the assault would simply go on and on, she nodded like some beaten animal surrounded by wolves.

"Of course you do." Haddard stroked her sweating throat. "But you will remain where I say you must. Bor?"

When, for the first time in what felt like days, she looked at Bor, she wasn't surprised to see he'd become less substantial. In a dim way she realized her aroused condition was responsible, but how could she hate a man who might become mist?

"Place it in her. Leave her thus while we eat."

Leave her impaled on the trainer! Suddenly afraid, she wrenched this way and that as best she could. Perhaps Bor sensed her desperation because he suddenly stepped back, holding the *trainer* which glistened with her fluids.

"Bor!" Haddard demanded. "I have spoken."

"What more do you want of her?"

Nearly undone by what she longed to believe was Bor's concern, she continued to stare at him even though his attention was now on his liege-lord. "She has had enough," Bor said in a low voice.

"Not nearly," Haddard countered. "Listen to me. You do not fully know why she is here. Neither of us does. When she speaks, I must know she holds back nothing."

"Ask her now."

"No! I am not ready."

Although she felt like shattered ice, she forced herself to turn Haddard's words around in her mind. Because she indeed knew something she suspected Haddard had kept to himself, she wondered if he feared her knowledge. If so, why didn't he simply kill her?

Because he first needed to learn things from her.

Bor, let me speak! Even if my words change the Kebo, it is time for the truth.

As if reading her thoughts, Bor stepped beside her and untied her gag. He threw it to the ground.

"No!" Haddard bellowed. "How dare you disobey me?"

"I will no longer do this." Bor hurtled the *trainer* against the wall. It slid to the floor and lay there. "She is a warrior, not a whore. I learned that during our time together and will not have her treated as one."

Haddard started shaking but whether from rage or fear she didn't know. As the Kebo leader glared, Bor released the ropes around her legs and drew them together. Pain from the improved circulation caused her to moan. She was still dealing with that when Bor freed her arms. She needed no encouragement to straighten and let her hands drop to her lap. Like her legs, her arms now throbbed and burned. Despite the discomfort, however, her pussy continued to command her attention.

Feeling as if she barely had control over her now-free body, she concentrated on opening and closing her hands and flexing her feet. Bor knelt beside her, a hand on her thigh.

"You defy me!" Haddard pulled a short knife out of the waistband holding his loincloth in place and pointed it toward her and Bor. "I chose you as war-liege in part because of your loyalty and belief in Lifelight. The captive has changed you."

"Perhaps." Bor started to massage her leg, his touch gentle yet deep as he probed cramped muscles. "But you too have changed, my lord. You fear her. I have never seen you afraid."

Instead of putting his weapon to use, Haddard paced from one end of the *mogan* to the other. When she'd first seen him, Nuwaa had been struck by his size and strength, which was unusual for a man who'd seen so many seasons, but he now looked diminished. She almost felt sorry for him.

Haddard stopped before a carving depicting wolves and eagles. Sinking to his knees, he first caressed the image, then, as Bor had done, he lowered his forehead to the ground. Although Bor continued to touch her, his attention was fixed on his liege-lord.

She hated this! Hated what she had to say.

Haddard's prayer reached her as little more than rumblings in a man's throat. She'd never known there could be a place like this, a shelter where everything sacred to a clan was kept together. The air felt heavy and rich and otherworldly. She needed to concentrate on that and ask herself what these objects and images meant to the Kebo and why her clan had nothing like it, but her body still wept, and Bor's touch reminded her of the too-few nights when his body had dried those tears.

Grunting from the effort, Haddard again stood up. He still held his knife which dangled from his fingers.

"Tell him," he whispered.

Despite the order, for a long time she couldn't make her throat work. Bor seemed in no hurry to hear what she had to say. Much as she wanted to lean against him, she didn't dare.

"I have seen your liege-lord before," she began. "I lived with him. Belonged in his world."

"What?" Bor's fingers ground into her flesh. "How can that be?"

"Because there are two men with nearly the same features, nearly the same voice."

Bor gave her an uncomprehending look, and she knew she could no longer try to spare him. "Bor, you told me you had a brother who was born at the same time you were. The two of you shared the same skin and thoughts. And when he died, part of you died."

"Yes."

"You are not the only one." She drew a deep breath to help her continue. "Your liege-lord too, has a twin, although they are not halves of a whole."

"What?"

"My Liege-lord Radislay."

Her words hadn't completely drifted away when Haddard buried his face in his hand. The gesture lasted only a moment, but by the time he'd straightened, she understood a great deal about soul-deep regret.

"I do not understand," she said because neither man seemed capable of speaking. "You and my liege-lord were born of the same parents. Why are you not together?"

Liege-lord Haddard's eyes burned into her.

"Why does my liege-lord hate you so?"

"Your twin leads the Sakar?" Bor demanded. "Again and again you told your people that the Sakar are our enemy and must be destroyed. But you never said why you felt this way."

"I hoped I would never have to."

"To hate one's brother..." Bor had been staring at his liege-lord, but he now turned his attention to her. His eyes left no doubt that what he'd just said was beyond his comprehension. Remembering what he'd told her of his deep love for his brother, she ached for him. If she dared, she would have embraced him, but her body continued to throb with need, and she didn't trust herself.

"From childhood we were enemies," Haddard whispered. "Even as young boys I knew he hated me."

"Why?" she asked.

Haddard shrugged. "Perhaps we were born knowing we could not share the same land. I remember our mother tried to place us both on her lap, but the moment I felt him next to me, I tried to push him away. He did the same, and we fought. We always fought."

"I loved my brother," Bor said.

"I know." She thought she saw regret in the older man's eyes, but it was gone so soon she couldn't be sure. "Perhaps our fighting made us mighty warriors because as we left childhood, we knew that no other could match our strength. I knew I could not trust him and learned to study his every move, his every word. Those things taught me how to see deep inside not just him, but all men. And women." He looked pointedly at her. "But my knowledge was not enough."

"What happened?" Bor asked.

"Our father was liege-lord of the Sakar. When he could no longer lead, leadership would fall to one of us. Only one."

She tried to imagine parents having to choose between their sons, but because Radislay's parents had died before she'd been brought to live with the Sakar, she didn't know what kind of people they'd been.

"One day the Sakar shaman and war-liege came to my father and told him that only one of his sons could continue to be called a Sakar. The other..."

Because Haddard now lived among the Kebo, she guessed that the leaders had demanded that one be cast from the clan. Haddard became a man without a birth clan, just as she was. She almost felt sorry for him.

"You were born a Sakar?" Bor's voice carried resignation.

"Yes," Haddard whispered. "But on the day our father handed us spears and told my brother and me to make the decision, I ceased to be one."

"You both lived," she managed. "You did not fight?"

"I was ready to. I knew that without my clan and the leadership that was mine by birthright that I would rather be dead. We went off by ourselves because we did not want anyone to see our battle. We each wounded and were wounded. We fought on and on, bleeding, resting a little, attacking again."

"And in the end?" Bor prompted.

"In the end I could no longer lift my spear. It was night. I ran."

Although a little illumination reached the sacred *mogan*, Nuwaa felt as if she'd been robbed of all sunlight. When Haddard spoke, she could think of nothing else, but now he'd fallen silent and was staring at each of the objects the Kebo considered sacred in turn. She'd seen the look in the eyes of a vanquished enemy, a soul-death coming even before the enemy warrior had breathed his last. Although she understood that Bor would want to keep his own emotions to himself, she turned her attention to him. He'd stood up without her noticing and now balanced his weight on spread and powerful legs. He felt so distant.

"And you found the Kebo," Bor whispered. "Instead of telling us the truth, you made us believe that you had been sent by Lifelight and would become our liege-lord."

Haddard's head jerked up. The sorrow of a moment before was gone, replaced by a fierceness she couldn't comprehend. "The Kebo are great because of me!" he thundered. "Before I came, they were like insects flying about without reason. They knew nothing of Lifelight's power and worshipped false gods, not these." He swept his arm around the *mogan*. "I gave the Kebo something to believe in. Now we Kebo are feared and respected by all clans. Our warriors are mighty because of me."

It was all too much for her. Even though she should have concerned herself with Bor's reaction, she couldn't think past her own shock. Gathering what was left of her strength, she grabbed her skirt and stood up. Her fingers shook as she put back on part of what made her a warrior. Covering her crotch made her feel less vulnerable, less connected to Bor. She'd never wanted to be alone more than she did right now so started toward the door.

"Where are you going?" Bor asked.

His words stopped her, but she didn't make the mistake of facing him. "What happens between you and Haddard is not part of me. I do not want to hear the words you speak to each other."

"Wait!" Haddard demanded. "Tell him."

"Tell me what?" Bor asked when she couldn't make herself move.

"Why she allowed herself to be captured."

Everything tumbled in her mind, and she felt sick, betrayed by her leader. When she faced Bor she saw betrayal in his eyes and knew they'd always share that one emotion, but it wasn't enough. "So I could kill the Kebo leader."

Chapter Thirteen

Nuwaa felt the heat of two men's eyes. She wondered if Bor would kill her before she reached his liege-lord, but maybe, like her, he needed solitude more than anything.

"Today I do not hear my lord's command," she told Haddard although she intended for Bor to hear as well. "The time may come when I regret my action, but just as you lied to those who became your people, so have I been lied to."

"Because your liege-lord did not tell you everything about who he was sending you to kill?" Bor asked.

Not trusting herself to speak, she nodded. Listening to her heart's erratic beat, she remembered what she'd been going to do and started toward the thick bark door again. This time no one spoke.

Stepping outside, she hardened herself against reacting to the feel of fresh air on her naked breasts and the image of the warrior she'd left. After a moment she realized that many eyes were on her. Her gaze settled on those who'd been her captors over the past few days, especially Durc, who was walking toward her.

"You are free," he said. His stance said he wasn't about to let her leave.

"Yes."

"Our liege-lord..."

"He released me."

Durc frowned and glanced at the sacred *mogan*. "I do not know whether to take your words as the truth. If you have cast a spell over him—"

"Bor was in there too," someone said. "I saw him."

Durc looked even more confused. "And he too said you could leave? After what took place between the two of you, he wants no more of you?"

I do not know. I could not see into his heart.

"Ask him," she managed.

Durc took another step toward her so that if he wanted, he could have easily captured her. "I have followed my war-liege for many seasons," he told her. "At times I am like a young buck challenging a great stag, but I always bow before his strength. Before I can let you leave, I must know it is as he wishes."

"It is."

Bor's voice turned her around. She saw what everyone else did, a stag among lesser beings, but he was even more than that to her. She alone knew what his body felt like during the moment of climax. He'd handed her his grief at his twin's death just as she'd handed him her tears in the wake of Tabathi's death. They'd slept wrapped around each other, fucked and fed, felt alive and given life.

And now his words had ended that.

"You do not want her?" Durc asked.

"Let her return to her people."

His words were heavy with meaning she barely comprehended, but even if she stayed until she did, it wouldn't change what he'd just said so she picked up her top and weapons and walked away.

Bor didn't move until he could no longer see Nuwaa. Then he ordered his warriors to meet with him. Instead of having them gather around the council fire, he led them away from the rest of the village. As he walked, he struggled not to think about his heavy balls and limp penis or the image of Nuwaa's retreating back.

He waited until the warriors were seated in a semicircle around him then told them everything he'd learned. He hadn't known what to expect and had tried to prepare himself for accusations that he was lying. Instead, no one spoke until he'd finished.

"Liege-lord Haddard did not deny anything she said?" Durc asked.

"No. In truth, he gave her permission to speak of what perhaps he could not. And once she had spoken of his twin, Haddard told us why he no longer calls himself a Sakar."

"Born a Sakar," someone muttered. "Born our enemy."

"But were they our enemy before Haddard came to live with us?" Bor questioned. "Or when the stranger who said he was sent by the gods told us to hate the Sakar, did we do so?"

Several of the older warriors remembered when Haddard hadn't lived among them, but their memories were hazy and, Bor suspected, tinged with Haddard's ability to make people believe what he'd wanted them to. His head throbbed. He wanted to tell himself his pain was because he could no longer revere his liege-lord, but that wasn't the only reason.

Nuwaa had walked away.

"Lies," Durc said, putting an end to the muttering. "Everything we believed about our gods are lies. They do not exist."

He couldn't believe that. Every clan he'd ever come in contact with had its gods that they relied on for courage and survival. Most either believed in Lifelight or a god of gods with another name but the same power. Careful to keep his tone neutral so each man could make up his own mind, he told his warriors that. Slowly, one by one, they nodded. Some held necklaces made from the carcasses of creatures they'd taken as their spirits while Rasja reminded everyone that without Sun God everything would grow cold and die. Durc, who never prayed unless he was going into battle, spoke of being visited by a giant white bird while on his vision quest. Instead of attacking him, the bird had plucked a feather from its chest and dropped it at Durc's feet.

"Our liege-lord is not who we believed him to be," Durc said, echoing Bor's thoughts. "But he brought truth with him and made us a clan."

"He also brought danger." Everyone turned toward Rasja who stood and joined Bor. "Haddard's brother sent a Kebo warrior to kill him. If she had not fallen under our war-liege's spell, she would have completed her mission."

"She would have tried," Durc amended. "Tell us, Bor. You would have stopped her then? Killed her if you had to?"

* * * * *

The discussion about what they needed to do took what was left of the day but finally Bor knew what was in everyone's heart. Although they wanted to hear the truth from Haddard's own lips, their belief in the man they'd always called their liege-lord had been destroyed. Whatever happened next, the clan had been fundamentally changed.

This wouldn't have happened if he hadn't brought Nuwaa here. If she'd died during the attack or he'd killed her or kept her a silent captive, his people wouldn't be facing what they now were. The responsibility he must bear weighed down on him as he led the way to the sacred *mogan*. The women and children and even the slave-whores watched the warriors' every step, and he knew he'd eventually have to tell them what he'd told the warriors.

For now though —

"Go in to him," Durc said. "Bring him out here where he is not surrounded by sacred objects. Make him a man like all other men."

Hating his task almost as much as he hated himself tonight, Bor pulled the door covering aside and stepped into the room that had always both awed and strengthened him. He heard no sound, and the light from a nearly spent burning branch hanging from the wall soon told him what his senses already had. Haddard wasn't here. Even more telling, the bear cape he wore as symbol of his leadership lay on the blanket that had held the tail he must have used to whip Nuwaa. When he picked up the cape, he thought, not of the message Haddard had left behind about relinquishing leadership, but what he'd allowed Haddard to do to Nuwaa.

Feeling old, heavy, and empty, he carried the cape outside and held it up so everyone could see.

"He is gone," Rasja said. "He will not return."

"No," Bor agreed.

"And the Kebo are without their spirit-leader," Durc added.

That caused a number of women to gasp. A crying baby fell silent. Looking around at everyone, Bor accepted the expectancy and trust in their eyes. He held the cape aloft. As one, the Kebo nodded.

He slipped it on. Accepted its weight and impact on the rest of his life.

*****

Bor knew his people expected him to sleep in the sacred *mogan*, but he needed to be alone with his thoughts tonight instead of surrounded by symbols of gods. His throat felt sore from repeating the truth about Haddard, and although he was hungry, he'd needed solitude more than he had food. When he'd told the warriors that he intended to sleep under the stars so he'd be as close as possible to his spirit, Durc had pushed one of the slave-whores at him.

"Prayers can wait," Durc had said. "First you need to silence your cock."

He'd slid his hands over the slave-whore's trembling body, even running a hand between her legs to feel her warm moisture, but his cock had continued to feel dead.

"*She* will not return." Durc shook his head as if reading his mind. "*She* is Sakar."

He knew that in every fiber of his being. Yet as he now lay staring up at the stars, he wondered whether his heart would ever hear the message.

His heart?

Bor sat up then positioned himself on his knees. His parents had told him that their hearts beat as one, and when his twin had been killed, his own heart had shattered. After burying his son, his father had gone off by himself for a number of days, but his mother had remained to weep in the village surrounded by family and friends.

"He does what he needs to," she'd said of her husband. "He will return with the other half of our heart when he feels strong enough." Then she'd surprised Bor by taking his face in her hands, something she hadn't done since he'd started living with other warriors-in-training. "I fear you will never experience what your father and I have," she'd whispered. "If you become war-liege as I believe you have the greatness for, that will be first in your life. No woman's heart will reach beyond your responsibilities."

"You were right," he said although he was speaking more to himself than his dead mother. "No woman shares my heart."

Strengthened by what he told himself was the truth, he let his hands stray to his cock. It didn't respond to his touch, but instead of releasing it, he continued to work it because if it came to life, maybe he'd stop thinking about anything else.

Nuwaa was on her way back to the Sakar. She didn't know what Haddard had done and probably didn't care. He wondered what she'd say when she confronted her liege-lord which he had no doubt she'd do.

His penis twitched, but instead of feeling encouraged, he groaned at the proof of the power Nuwaa held over him. He told himself it wouldn't last long. As soon as he'd met individually with the warriors, he'd ask the clan's shaman and most spiritual members for guidance. He wasn't sure how to be a liege-lord, but he had to accept the role because his clan's safety and future depended on it.

A sound many might take for the wind pulled him away from his swirling thoughts. The sound which was nothing more than faint pressure on the ground was repeated.

"Durc?"

The warrior he'd decided to have take his place as war-liege didn't respond. Besides, the pressure was too light for him. A slave-whore?

"Go," he said. "I do not want you."

"But I need you."

His flesh heated. He forgot to breathe. "Nuwaa?"

Up until this moment, Nuwaa hadn't quite comprehended that she'd made the decision to return to the Kebo. No, not the Kebo, she amended when Bor repeated her name. Tonight she wanted to see only one person.

"You are alone?" she asked. Standing deep in the brush was easier than walking into the clearing where the moon would bathe her.

"Yes. How did you find me?"

How could she tell him about letting her feet go where her heart directed? "I do not— Bor?"

"What?"

"Did my leaving cause much trouble for you?"

"That is why you came back?"

No. Yes. I do not know. "I have been surrounded by Kebo for days and nights. I should want them to be nothing to me as they have always been, but I can no longer believe that." She hated sounding so confused but didn't know how to change the truth. "Has Haddard taken his anger out on you? Is that why you are out here?"

"Come here, please."

Please. Barely believing what she was doing, she stepped closer. He'd removed his necklace and wore nothing more than his loincloth. Despite herself, she studied what she could see of what it covered, but in the dim light she couldn't tell whether he had an erection. Seeing and hearing him had brought her own body back to life. She didn't try to tell herself that what she'd been forced to endure earlier today had anything to do with her condition because she knew the simple truth. Her body wanted his.

Wanted. Only wanted.

"Sit down," he said softly, his words reminding her that she was standing over him. Instead of settling onto the spot he'd indicated, she looked down at him thinking of how strange it felt to be taller and more prepared for battle than he was.

But she'd never battle him again.

And after tonight she'd never see him again.

"Why are you here?" she finally thought to ask and then sank to her knees. Although she was close enough to touch him she didn't try. Neither did he reach for her.

"I needed to be with my thoughts. Much has changed since you left."

"What? Haddard—"

"No longer lives among us."

"I do not understand." She stifled the urge to look around and see if Haddard might be nearby and preparing to run a weapon into her.

Her concern died as soon as Bor started speaking, and she remained motionless while he told her what had taken place. To her surprise, she found herself feeling sorrow for Haddard and told Bor so.

"Why, after what he did to you?"

"He was cast out of his birth home and now is homeless again."

"He abused you."

"Yes."

"And I let it happen."

"Yes."

Her word hung between them, growing heavier and heavier with each passing heartbeat.

"Thank you for coming here," he whispered and touched her knee. "I needed our last words to each other to be healing ones."

"So did I," she admitted and took his hand. She laced her fingers through his, his strength sliding into her. "Do you want to become liege-lord of the Kebo?"

"I will do what I must for my people." He pulled her hand toward him and rested it against his warm chest. "Much will change for me."

"You will no longer call yourself a warrior and leader of warriors."

"No."

She couldn't tell whether he felt regret and wouldn't ask because if he wanted her to know, he'd tell her. But it would have to happen tonight.

"I am still a warrior," she said. Then, although she hadn't known she was going to do so, she slid around so she could lean against him. He placed his arms over her shoulder and held her close. *Warrior? What was that?*

"Is it what you want?" he asked. "You are ready to take up a spear and protect and perhaps die for your people?"

"My people?" She tried to turn the word around in her mind, but his heat was distracting her. "The Sakar became my clan," she admitted. "But I was not born to them. Because my hair and eyes are darker, and I do not know who my parents are, I can never forget that my blood is different from theirs, just like Haddard."

"Do not speak of him!" Perhaps regretting his outburst, he started stroking her back. The sensation was one she'd never felt before and had never allowed herself to want. "Tonight nothing exists except you and me. We will not speak of tomorrow."

Of my leaving and your new role.

"I want you," she admitted and ran her fingers down his side. "Not just to fuck but so I will have something to remember of our time together."

"I wish I could give you my seed to grow inside you."

Tears sprang to her eyes. Lost in her reaction, she could only hug him.

"But it will not happen because Sakar warrior-women take the herbs which prevent pregnancy, do they not?" he said. "Haddard did not lie to us about that, did he?"

"No. It is better this way," she tried to tell both of them. "The child of the Kebo leader should not be raised as a Sakar never knowing its father. Bor, what happened?"

"What do you mean?"

She tried to pull back so she could look into his eyes, but he wouldn't let her. Instead of feeling under his control, she felt safe and protected, maybe even loved. At the same time, thoughts of how much she'd been changed by him frightened her. She was a warrior. She'd never been anything else and didn't know how.

Then he covered a breast with his large and competent hand, and she thought of little else. "You believe something happened between us?" he asked.

"I do not... Yes."

"What?"

You stopped being the enemy, stopped being my captor. "Do not ask me that!"

"Then do not ask me either."

She almost laughed, but so much of her had flowed into him that she couldn't concentrate on anything else. Straightening, she pushed on his chest until he fell back. He lay with his arms at his side, knees bent, looking up at her. When he reached for her, she leaned forward so he could draw her down on top of him. Her cheek briefly rested on his chest, but because tonight would have to last for the rest of her life, she turned her head so she could place her mouth over his pectoral muscle. His skin tasted of salt and smoke and male. Suddenly hungry, she tongued his nipple while he stroked her arms. Over and over again she sucked what she could of his muscled flesh into her. The sensation traveled hot and heavy down her body, and her cunt began heating in anticipation of when that opening would be filled.

Their legs were now intertwined. She didn't know or care how that had happened. All that mattered was the feel of him, the layers of fabric between them. As much as she wanted flesh kissing flesh, she loved the anticipation.

Slow and easy as if asking permission, he rolled her over and onto her back so their positions were now reversed. His mouth embraced her breast, dampening her hard nipple. She felt her flesh being sucked into him. This was nothing like being a captive because she gave freely of herself. When he cupped the base of her breast to bring even more of it within reach of his mouth, she signaled her pleasure by running her fingers up and down his forearm. Her other hand went around his neck, finding the top of his spine and holding him to her.

He nipped and nibbled, bathed and sucked until her breast became so sensitive that pleasure started to slide into something else. But before she was forced to find a way to let him know, he released her and pushed himself up on his elbows so he could look down at her. Her legs were now cradled within his, her cunt trapped by her own flesh but not silenced.

"You are beautiful," he whispered. "When I look at you I think of morning sun on a new flower."

No one had ever said anything like that to her. She'd been praised for her enthusiasm during sex and her courage in battle but never had she thought she'd hear those words or want to.

"You are too," she told him which caused him to chuckle. She felt the deep rumble down her length before it settled against and in her cunt. If only they were naked!

"If you think I am beautiful then you must ask your spirit for new eyes."

Joining him in this strange thing called laughter, she wrapped her arms around him and rolled him under her so she now lay on top. Sliding down his body a little, she rested her head against his chest. Even as her clit throbbed, she wondered if she could spend the night as his blanket.

"Do you ache?" he asked, his hands reaching as best they could for her buttocks.

"Ache?"

"In your cunt? The trainer..."

What she felt had nothing to do with discomfort. Still, knowing he cared brought her too close to tears. Maybe he sensed her struggle because he pushed her up and stared into her eyes. "I let him hurt and tease you," he told her. "Everything in me raged against what Haddard was doing and what I did, but for too long I did not stop."

"Because you are Kebo and I am Sakar," she managed even though speaking carried hints of her tears.

"Not tonight."

"No, not tonight."

She thought he was going to let her lower herself back onto him. Instead, he guided her off him and lay her on her side next to him. When he sat up, she tried to do the same, but he slid his hands under her hips and turned her she was now fully on her back. She couldn't see enough of his expression as he pulled off her skirt, but it didn't matter because his hands spoke of tenderness and that was enough. Still wearing his loincloth, he positioned himself on his knees between her legs, then lifted hers so they now rested on his thighs. When he spread his fingers over her hipbones, she felt as if she was melting into both him and the fur under her. More relaxed maybe than she'd been in her entire life, she placed her hands under her head.

She trusted him.

Awe and acceptance spread over her in equal waves. His hands began making soft, gliding movements starting with her hips but continuing to her belly, mons, thighs, and weeping pussy. She couldn't keep her hips still. They thrust toward him over and over again, lacking rhythm. He touched his thumbs to her clit, his gentleness briefly calming her. Then he turned his life-roughened fingers to her swollen lips and she felt herself gliding into his touch, losing herself, hungry and willing to surrender everything to him.

"Do you hurt here?" He touched a fingertip to her clit.

Gasping, she shook her head. "Not hurt."

"But the way I punished—"

"Not punishment," she corrected. "From someone else, yes, it would have been."

He made a sound she couldn't fathom and slid a finger inside her, just barely penetrating but full of promise. "But from me?"

"I loved what—" Fear of how much she was on the verge of revealing stopped her, but he already knew so much and had done so much. "I felt as if I had handed myself to you. I was helpless, but I did not hate it. I wanted, needed..."

Maybe he understood what she was trying to say. Maybe he understood the limits of words. And perhaps, like her, he no longer cared about speech.

As she stared up at the stars and a soft night breeze played with her breasts, he painted her core with fingers made wet by her juices. Deliberately breathing slow and deep, she existed nowhere except where he touched. She'd handed herself over to him, and he understood the gift. One moment his attention centered around her lips as if he'd never get enough of exploring them. The next he slipped into her, sometimes with a single finger, sometimes filling her. Her buttocks and hips continued their telling and disjointed movements.

"I do not want you to come yet," he whispered. "When you do, I want it to happen as one."

She was trying, but she now knew she'd waited her entire life to find a man she felt safe entrusting her body to. It tore at her to know this wouldn't last, and she couldn't handle her grief any way except by losing herself in her body and what Bor knew about it.

"No ropes," he continued. Now two fingers rested within her while he pressed on her lower pelvis as if trying to get his hands to join. Caught between his fingers, she struggled to listen. "Remember, the last time we were together, there were no ropes."

"Do not, please. I cannot think of that."

"Neither can I."

Exhausted by the words, she tried to take her thoughts no further than what his hands were accomplishing, but he abruptly abandoned her to yank off his loincloth. He threw it into the dark, and she stared openly, drunkenly at his cock.

"Now," she whimpered. "Please, now."

Nodding, he drew her legs up against her belly so her ass was lifted before scooting closer. His cock instantly found her entrance and pressed against it for a moment before slipping in. Moaning, she once again simply existed while he gripped her bent knees and used his leverage to begin pumping. She caressed his hands, arms, thighs, every part of him she could touch but was barely aware of what she was doing because this man, this liege-lord of the Kebo, had housed himself in her woman's place.

She had come back, not so she could learn what had happened among the Kebo, but because her hunger had been this great. She'd hold him in her, hold and cradle and shelter him, bounce and shudder under his assault, sweat and groan with him. Her cunt would drink of him and quench his thirst. He'd asked her not to come until he was ready so she commanded her senses to flow into him. She settled deep within his mind and heart, muscles, and blood. He existed not just against her ass and over her legs but everywhere.

Deeper and deeper he drove into her. Each slight withdrawal felt like a small death, but she survived because she knew he'd offer more and more. Her head filled, muscles melted only to grow strong. She loved his cock's gliding, milking motions. It heated her and engorged her veins and sent her muscles to quivering. They clenched, clenched again, trembled and shook. She sobbed out his name over and over. He slammed against her and pinned her with his body. She heard him say her name, the sound hard and soft at the same time, echoing throughout her.

When, finally, her climax had spent itself, she collapsed. He too felt boneless but remained wrapped around her, his cock cradled in the home she provided.

Chapter Fourteen

Bor woke to find his world still dark and Nuwaa on her side next to him. He thought she was sleeping, but although he wanted to return to the nothing place she resided in, having her arm around him made that impossible.

In the morning she'd go back where she belonged, and he'd return to his village to begin the work of healing his people. All they had was tonight.

"Nuwaa," he whispered so perhaps the night creatures wouldn't hear. "I want to taste you."

She stirred and snuggled closer. "I want to taste you," he repeated. After a moment he felt strength slide into her body and knew she was awake.

"And I want to drink of you," she told him.

Because he'd never thought of how a woman might pleasure him while he was lapping her fluids, at first he didn't know how to satisfy both their needs but soon learned that by their laying head to legs, she could play with his cock while he worked his tongue in and out of her opening. She had to hook a leg over his head which made him feel trapped at first, but as she ran her tongue over and over his cock, he stopped thinking about that. Unfortunately, because of his greater height, he had to curve his body around her. Besides, giving and receiving at the same time took more concentration than he had.

She must have felt the same way because she lifted her leg and scooted away from him. After turning around, she settled her body down between his legs and began licking his penis. Fisting his hand in her hair, he willed his thoughts to go no further than what she was doing to him. He, who had nearly forgotten what it was like when he didn't lead men into battle, had turned himself over to a woman he'd always considered the enemy. After acknowledging that he'd never feel her teeth against his sensitive skin again, he gave himself up to her—and to his trust of her. Heat prickled and sometimes grew so intense he thought he'd explode, but she seemed to know how far to push him because when he neared the peak, her tongue caresses turned from a sharp wind to the gentlest of breezes. He floated under her manipulations like a leaf in a wide current.

Finally she lifted her head. "Now it is my turn," she whispered.

Although he had to work at pushing life back into his muscles, he finally managed to place himself so his head was between her splayed legs. With her legs resting on his shoulders and back, he had easy access. He touched and teased with his tongue, bathing mons, lips, the tiny, hard bud. As he worked her he wondered if he could keep her taste with him for the rest of his life.

The rest of his life.

Unable to keep the thought at bay, he sat up and then pulled her up beside him. "Will this be enough for you?" he asked. "A night of fucking and you are ready to walk away?"

"I must."

"Must?"

"The Sakar must know what the Kebo do, that their liege-lords are responsible for the hatred between our clans."

"And when you have?"

"I am a warrior. It is all I have ever been. I need to ask my liege-lord why he was ready to throw my life away so he could have his revenge." Her voice became hard. "I have given him everything—my loyalty, my courage. My body."

He clenched his teeth at the thought.

"Bor, Radislay made me into what I am. I do not know how to be anything else."

"Neither do I," he admitted. "But now I must become something else—leader of the Kebo."

"You will be a good liege-lord," she said. He tried to understand why her voice shook, but the weight in his heart made that impossible. "One who does not need to keep his true self hidden from his people, one who is not driven by hatred and regret."

What he regretted in ways he barely comprehended was not being able to offer her what she needed most, peace of the spirit.

When he took her face in his hands and brought his mouth close to hers, she tensed momentarily. Then she turned soft and yielding, trusting. They kissed, not just in passion but driven by something deeper and soul-felt. Instead of crushing her mouth beneath his, he kept the touch as gentle as butterfly wings. She returned his touch with one that was the same and sighed softly. Slowly, wonderfully, the pressure increased. He parted his lips, and she did the same. Unsure of how to kiss her as a man kisses a woman, he turned his head first one way and then the other. Their noses bumped, and they laughed. She ran her fingers over the sides of his neck. Because he still held her face, they shared control. She tasted of woman, of life. Her lips felt as soft as her pussy, damp and warm.

I love you. I will always love you.

* * * * *

Nuwaa wasn't sure, but she thought she and Bor had sex three more times before morning. Because his body never left hers, and she dozed between climaxes, she wasn't certain where one joining ended and another began. She became insatiable, drinking of him even when she didn't know how he managed to continue to answer her need to be fucked. Maybe, like her, he needed enough sex to last a lifetime.

As dawn kissed the world, she lifted a leg from its resting place over his hip and slid out from under him. His hand glided from her back to her waist, then to her breast, and although she needed to pee, she stopped moving. He simply rested his fingers over her breast, so she took hold of his wrist and brought his hand to her lips so she could tattoo his palm and fingers with tiny kisses.

She'd never spent an entire night with a man and had certainly never used her body to thank a man for gifting her as he'd done. Her mind briefly touched on how she'd satisfy her sexual urges once she returned to her people, but maybe that part of her would die once she'd left him.

I love you. You have changed me, and I love you for it.

Frightened by the thought, by her weakness, she stood. She sensed him watching as she walked away. After relieving herself, she forced herself to return but didn't speak as she put back on her skirt and picked up the knife he'd given her.

He was a Kebo, she a Sakar.

"I leave," she said with her back to him so he couldn't see her tears and she didn't have to look at him. "Return to your people. Lead them into tomorrow."

"Tell your liege-lord they have nothing to fear from the Kebo. We will never attack again."

"Thank you," she whispered. Then because she knew she couldn't leave like this after all, she turned around. He lay on the pelt, his war-honed body powerful even at rest. "It would be easier if we had never met," she told him. "I would know who I am and not question my life, my beliefs."

"You and I are not responsible for the hatred that has always existed between our clans, but we must live with the consequences."

"If things had been otherwise, we might have come together as equals, not captive and captor."

"Nuwaa? I am sorry. The things I did to you—"

She waved him off. "I, a Sakar, attacked you and your fellow warriors."

"Because your liege-lord commanded you to."

And she'd obeyed because of who and what she was and had always been. Feeling overwhelmed by what felt like endless mountains between them, she simply nodded. "With you as their leader, the Kebo will succeed as they never have before."

"Be careful," he whispered. "And when you return to your people, find peace."

Overwhelmed by emotion, she walked into the wilderness.

Chapter Fifteen

The season of harvest had reached its final days. Mornings were cold, and frost coated the ground. As he stood in the now empty sacred *mogan* for the last time, Bor knew he'd waited longer than he should have to move his clan to the lush valley the warriors had found earlier. He'd told himself he hadn't wanted to rush the leave-taking because this area had served them well, but although no one had questioned his decision, he knew the truth.

This was where he and Nuwaa had slept together for the last time. They'd seen each other as equals here, and their lives had changed in this spot.

But the rest of the Kebo were on their way to their winter home, and he needed to join them.

Still, he paused at the opening to the *mogan* and let memories have their way with him. Although he hated the memories of what he'd subjected her to within these walls, he didn't deny them because that was also the day so much had changed for both of them. Lifelong beliefs had crumbled. The man he'd always thought of as a god had turned out to be a fraud.

It didn't matter because since Haddard had walked away, he and the rest of the clan had begun to forge new beliefs out of what was good and strong about what Haddard had brought to them when they were little more than savages. Even Haddard's family had chosen the clan over him.

When he turned his back to the *mogan*, his thoughts left Haddard and his impact on the Kebo and turned, as they often did, to Nuwaa. She was strong and brave. He had no doubt that she'd confronted her liege-lord and could imagine her standing before him demanding he tell the clan why they'd spent so long thinking of the Kebo as their enemy. If Radislay had been as honest as his brother had, the Sakar might have turned their backs on him and embraced a new liege-lord—maybe Nuwaa.

Was she now leader of her clan?

He tried to imagine her surrounded by symbols of her new status but the image wouldn't form. Instead he saw her naked and heated, arms and legs reaching for him, the smell of sex surrounding her, her lips seeking his.

"Bor."

For a heartbeat, he did nothing more than absorb the sound of her voice. His heart raced, and his face felt hot. Slow and uncertain, he turned. She stood a short distance away, dressed as a Sakar warrior, armed with knife and spear. He thought her magnificent.

"Nuwaa," he said.

"Where are your people?" she asked.

"On their way to their winter home, not the one Haddard wanted us to go to but a place without abuli."

"Good." A faint smile touched her mouth. "You are not with them."

"No."

"But you will be?"

"Soon."

Soon.

The longer she studied Bor, the less certain Nuwaa became. When she'd left the Sakar she'd thought of little except her destination. Now she was here but without the words to explain what had brought her. Maybe, she acknowledged, her hesitation came not from an inability to express herself but his body's impact on her senses.

"You are their leader?" she asked.

"Yes. What are you doing here?"

She should have been better prepared for the question. If she had been, she wouldn't be fighting the urge to run away. But she was a warrior, at least she'd never been anything else.

"I learned something about my beginning." Her throat closed down, momentarily rendering her speechless.

Maybe he sensed how hard this was for her because he quickly closed the distance between them and took her hands. When he placed her palms on his chest, her fingers absorbed his heat. The sensation was both familiar and new. Nearly overwhelming.

"Tell me," he encouraged.

Tell me. With him to draw courage from, she began by explaining that her route to the Sakar had taken her past the cave where she and her fellow warriors had attacked the Kebo. She'd discovered Tabathi's body, at least what animals hadn't eaten. The Sakar always carried their dead warriors home for prayers and burial, but although the two dead Sakar men were gone no one had bothered with Tabathi.

"I prayed for her soul," Nuwaa explained. "And piled rocks on her bones. I took some of her hair." She showed him the bracelet she'd woven from the long, white locks.

"Tabathi gave her life to the Sakar, but they did not see her as one of them."

"I am sorry, so sorry. It should not have been like that," he whispered, which gave her the courage to continue. She explained that when she'd returned to her people, her shocked-looking liege-lord had immediately insisted on speaking alone to her. He'd listened impatiently to everything that had happened to her since her capture, interrupting several times to hurry her along. She'd allowed herself to be rushed until she got to the moment when she'd stood face to face with Haddard.

"So," Radislay had said. "You saw."

"Yes."

"You understand?"

"That you and the liege-lord of the Kebo are brothers, yes."

"Have you told any Sakar?" he'd demanded.

"No. I wanted to speak to you first."

He'd looked suspicious and something else she'd read as a mix of anger and fear. "Did you complete your mission?" He'd grabbed her arms and yanked her close. "You killed him?"

"No."

At her word, he'd tried to shake her, but she'd pulled free. She'd seen his hand reach for his knife so had drawn her own before asking if he'd expected to see her again.

"You should be dead! You and *him*!"

"He is your brother, blood of your blood."

Radislay had spat. "Do not say that! He is the spawn of a jackal and the lowest of snakes. He fucks vultures."

"That is why you wanted me to kill him? Because—"

"Because only one of us should live."

She'd taken a moment to absorb that then returned to the question that had obsessed her. What had he expected to happen to her if she'd managed to kill his brother?

His lips had thinned and his grip on his knife had tightened. "The Kebo would have killed you," he'd said without emotion.

"My life meant nothing? Or maybe you were willing to sacrifice me so I could not tell the Sakar what I had learned about the Kebo liege-lord."

His eyes had provided the answer. And the knife being lifted toward her said nothing had changed. She'd stood her ground because she had more questions. Why had he chosen her for this devil's mission?

"I granted you life," he'd said. "Spared you when I could have killed you. You are mine to do with as I wish."

"Granted you life," Bor repeated. His question brought her back to the present. "What did he mean?"

She'd had days to reconcile herself to the truth, but sharing what she now knew still took all her courage. She pressed her fingers more firmly against Bor's chest and spoke with her eyes closed.

"When I was a small child, Sakar warriors led by Radislay attacked my birth clan. They waited until my clan's men were gone and slaughtered the women and children they found. Radislay pulled me out of my dying mother's arms—he'd slashed her throat—and took me with him."

The words had taken so much out of her that she'd finished before she realized Bor was stroking her hair.

"Some Sakar knew the truth," he said. "But no one ever spoke of the slaughter?"

"No."

"They robbed you of your birth, your blood."

"Yes."

"Because they wanted you useful to them."

He understood everything. "Yes."

"And when Radislay had placed everything before you, you knew you could no longer stay with the Sakar."

She needed to cry because maybe tears would ease the ache. But all the time she'd been walking here she hadn't cried and she wouldn't now. "Radislay wanted me dead," she managed. "If I had insisted on staying, one of us would have had to die."

"You are not one of them. You know nothing of your birth clan. Nuwaa, why did you come here?"

Opening her burning eyes, she leaned back and brought Bor into focus. "My body guided me. And my heart."

Nodding, he gently kissed her forehead. "My heart welcomes you home."

Beyond words, truly feeling as if she had come home, she pressed her breasts and hips against his. Folding his greater size around her, he held her close and warm while his cock expanded and her core heated.

They kissed over and over again. Hands roamed and painted, tested and learned. She didn't rush taking his cock in her fingers because she wanted him to know she loved everything about him and not just the part of him capable of giving her the greatest pleasure. He, too, caressed back, shoulders, waist and arms with gentle fingers. His mouth moved from her lips to her cheeks, nose, eyes, the side of her neck. When she needed to give him more, she lowered herself to her knees and took him into her mouth. As she stroked him with tongue and lips, he undid her hair and it fell over her shoulders.

Then he joined her on the ground where he slowly removed her clothes, and she did the same for him. Saying nothing, she leaned away from him and placed her arms behind her and spread her legs to welcome him in. He leaned over and around her, and his cock entered its home. Slowly, almost gently they fucked. Even when the wave overtook her, she remained more aware of his release than her own.

When they were done and resting in each other's arms, he asked if she was still taking the herbs to keep her from getting pregnant.

"No."

At her word, he touched his lips to hers. "Thank you."

Epilogue

Bor stood behind Nuwaa, rubbing the small of her back. "You do not look like a warrior," he teased. "You waddle when you walk, and you have not run for days."

"I will again," she retorted with mock severity. "And when I do I will leave you far behind."

"With our baby in your arms?"

Giving up on her attempt to make Bor believe pregnancy and motherhood wouldn't change her role as a warrior, she leaned against him, which caused him to stop rubbing her back and place his arms around her. They stood like that for several moments watching a number of Kebo warriors prepare for a hunting trip. Because the older woman who would attend her when she gave birth said the baby wasn't ready to be born, Bor would go with them. She wanted him to remain here with her, not because she still felt like an outsider when he wasn't by her side, but she loved it when he placed his hand on her belly so he could feel their child move.

At least the men were simply going out after the turkeys one of them had come across yesterday. When they returned, she'd join the other women in teasing them about being such poor hunters that they lacked the skill to kill anything other than slow-witted turkeys.

"You have spoken to Chise?" Bor asked. "She will nurse our baby so you can go with us when we search for a new home?"

"Of course." She shook her head. He wasn't yet a father and already he felt protective toward his son or daughter. But she wasn't angry because she understood that he still had a lot to learn about friendships between women.

Friendship. Although she now considered Chise and others her companions, she hadn't yet grasped the fullness the word signified. She'd thought it would take a long time, if ever, for the Kebo women to accept that a former Sakar warrior now slept with their liege-lord, but one by one they'd approached her, first to ask about the differences between how Kebo and Sakar women did things, then, when they'd learned she was pregnant, to tell her what to expect when she gave birth and how to care for an infant. As she'd grown more comfortable around them, she'd asked how they felt about the slave-whores.

It was the way of warriors, they told her, to frequently satisfy their urges. As long as their men didn't love a slave-whore, they didn't care.

Then she'd gone to Bor and talked to him about freedom. She hadn't needed to remind him that she understood what it was to be a captive. He'd listened to her and learned. Now, although some of the warriors grumbled, Liege-lord Bor had declared that any whores who wanted to leave could. Only two had.

"Do you miss it?" Her man indicated the hunting preparations. "Do you wish you were a slender, strong warrior again?"

"Sometimes," she admitted. The baby kicked, and she placed her hands over her belly. "But then I feel life inside me. I am ready to be what I did not have, a mother."

His hands traveled from her shoulders to her heavy breasts. "That is all you want now, to be a mother?"

"Yes," she whispered. Then, "One who nightly fucks the father of her children."

Enjoy this excerpt from
Scarlet Cavern
© Copyright Vonna Harper, 2004

All Rights Reserved, Ellora's Cave Publishing, Inc.

Shana stepped inside the nondescript door and reluctantly closed it behind her. The interior was too dark and quiet. Her every instinct screamed at her to return to the successful, in-control life she'd carved for herself, but of course she couldn't.

Until she'd learned whether Lindsay was dead or alive, nothing else mattered.

When her eyes adjusted to the gloom, she realized she was in a long, narrow hall. Recovery should have—what, certainly a more impressive looking office. She'd been led to believe the private organization had connections that put the FBI and Secret Service to shame, but she had her doubts. Shit, it had cost her a thousand dollars just to get information about Recovery. If the head of security for a precious gems' company had lied to her, she'd—what, sue the man while maybe Lindsay's life lay in the balance?

Thoughts of what might have happened to the woman she still considered her sister sent Shana down the hall. In the years since she and Lindsay had shared everything, she'd turned her body into a finely-honed tool and become the model she'd dreamed of back when Lindsay was living a nightmare. Most times she accepted her body as her meal ticket, but today she was grateful for her muscular legs, the product of endless hours in the gym and running track. If she didn't like what she saw about Recovery, she'd turn tail and run.

Only she couldn't.

Are you still alive, Lindsay? Please, you have to be!

The sign on the door at the end of the hall looked as if it had been nailed up by someone who'd never used a hammer before, but when she depressed the latch, she noted the door was steel. There were two deadbolts. As she stepped inside, she caught a humming sound. A bank of glowing monitors on a far wall explained a lot about the sound. Whoever was behind the San Diego branch of Recovery relied on high tech.

At first glance, the room looked empty, but that was because it was so large that taking it all in took time. There were several cubicles, each with its own computer. Intense, casually dressed men and women hunched over the units.

A thin middle-aged woman stood and walked toward her, her gaze never leaving Shana. "You're looking for Galen, right?" she said.

"I—yes, that's the name I was given."

"There." The woman pointed at a room to the left. "He's expecting you."

"Oh," Shana managed. She didn't know what she'd expected, maybe armed guards, maybe being frisked, something. Instead, no one seemed concerned that an outsider had walked into the middle of an ultra-secret organization. Then she realized everyone was watching her.

Could they feel her tension, her fear, the undeniable sexual excitement spawned by the unknown?

Turned on? Shit, Shana, are you insane!

Pretending indifference, she thanked the woman. Like the first one, this door was substantial, nearly impenetrable. This new room was maybe a tenth the size of the outer one and consisted of a large, cluttered desk with several well-worn easy chairs clustered around it. Behind the desk, nearly obscured by it, sat a man who couldn't have been more than five and a half feet tall. Like the woman out front, he'd said good-bye to his forties, and like the woman, his gaze locked on her. She was used to drawing attention and most times took it for what it was worth which wasn't much. But right now wasn't about her. Only Lindsay mattered.

The man had almost no hair and from its straggly appearance, he couldn't care less. His shirt looked as if he'd pulled it out of the dryer after it had sat there for days. His hands were large compared to the rest of him, and when he stood and came around the desk toward her, she wondered when he'd last bothered to eat.

"I'm Galen," he said, holding out his hand. "And you're Shana."

"Yes." He hadn't invited her to sit down so she continued to stand. The room smelled of old wood and dust, yet his computer setup looked as if a person could run the space program from it.

"All right, Shana, I know you have a lot of questions about Recovery, but first I want to give you an idea of how efficient we are. If you don't mind, I'd like to bring the operative you'll be working with in now."

The operative? Like a human being?

Before she could decide whether to make a point of the odd term, the door she'd just come through opened again, and a man filled the space. Hell, he did more than fill it, he commanded it.

His height? Well over six feet and as hard as a seasoned professional athlete. The black and silver Oakland Raiders logo T-shirt he wore seemed painted on muscle and bone. For a moment she couldn't take her eyes off the pirate figure in the middle of his chest. Was the man encased in the shirt the embodiment of the pirate, savage and aggressive—taker of things or people he desired?

An icy fist gripped her heart, making it hard to breathe. At the same time, she felt rawly alive. With an effort, she continued her appraisal. He stood with his legs slightly spread, impressive chest muscles forcing his arms out a bit from his body. He needed a shave. Surely once he'd run a razor over his chin he'd look less dark, less shadowed. Surely. He also needed a haircut although the unkempt length added to the uncivilized male look. His eyes were coal-black, deep-set and large—penetrating.

Speaking of penetrating—

All right, no way could she not notice the tale-tale bulge. Not notice nothing! If she didn't know better, she'd swear the damn thing was calling to her, challenging her to open her legs to it and let his cock consume her.

And he'd consume. Ream her out both physically and emotionally and leave her—leave her, what? *His?*

Suddenly scared, Shana forced her attention off the big, dark, maybe deadly male.

"Shana," Galen said. "This is Ranger."

Ranger? Doesn't he have a last name?

Shaking hands with Galen had been easy but no way in hell was she ready to let this...this animal-like creature touch her. She managed a nod at the still-silent man and sank into the nearest chair. She couldn't begin to relax. "What do you mean, operative?" she asked. Damn, her voice held a husky note, the voice of a woman turned on.

Galen looked at Ranger, obviously waiting for him to answer her question. When Ranger only continued his predator-like perusal of her, Galen sighed. "The web site you directed us to when you first contacted Recovery — the Scarlet Cavern — how much do you know about it?"

For an instant, all air seemed to leave the room. *This is important*, she thought. *Maybe the most important thing you'll do in your life. Life-changing.*

"Not much," she admitted in that sex-deepened tone. "Just what I saw from the public pages."

"Which are practically useless." Ranger spoke for the first time, his voice low and rough. "What's there gets past the morality patrol. Only those who have been allowed access get the real picture."

"And you have access?" she asked, cold again.

He nodded.

"In what context?" she demanded. When he only returned her stare, she switched her attention to Galen who struck her as being more tense than he'd been at the beginning. "All right, so all I have are the teasers to go by." She suppressed a shudder. "But what I saw — the short movie clips of my best friend being beaten — naked, tied and gagged…" She took a deep breath. "How much worse can it get?"

"Enough," Ranger muttered. He stepped all the way in the room and leaned against Galen's desk. He'd positioned himself, maybe deliberately, so his cock was nearly at her eye level. *Ignore that* he seemed to be saying.

About the author:

Vonna welcomes mail from readers. You can write to her c/o Ellora's Cave Publishing at 1337 Commerce Drive, Suite 13, Stow OH 44224.

Why an electronic book?

We live in the Information Age—an exciting time in the history of human civilization in which technology rules supreme and continues to progress in leaps and bounds every minute of every hour of every day. For a multitude of reasons, more and more avid literary fans are opting to purchase e-books instead of paperbacks. The question to those not yet initiated to the world of electronic reading is simply: *why?*

1. *Price.* An electronic title at Ellora's Cave Publishing and Cerridwen Press runs anywhere from 40-75% less than the cover price of the <u>exact same title</u> in paperback format. Why? Cold mathematics. It is less expensive to publish an e-book than it is to publish a paperback, so the savings are passed along to the consumer.

2. *Space.* Running out of room to house your paperback books? That is one worry you will never have with electronic novels. For a low one-time cost, you can purchase a handheld computer designed specifically for e-reading purposes. Many e-readers are larger than the average handheld, giving you plenty of screen room. Better yet, hundreds of titles can be stored within your new library—a single microchip. (Please note that Ellora's Cave and Cerridwen Press does not endorse any specific brands. You can check our website at www.ellorascave.com or

www.cerridwenpress.com for customer recommendations we make available to new consumers.)

3. *Mobility.* Because your new library now consists of only a microchip, your entire cache of books can be taken with you wherever you go.

4. *Personal preferences are accounted for.* Are the words you are currently reading too small? Too large? Too…**ANNOYING**? Paperback books cannot be modified according to personal preferences, but e-books can.

5. *Instant gratification.* Is it the middle of the night and all the bookstores are closed? Are you tired of waiting days—sometimes weeks—for online and offline bookstores to ship the novels you bought? Ellora's Cave Publishing sells instantaneous downloads 24 hours a day, 7 days a week, 365 days a year. Our e-book delivery system is 100% automated, meaning your order is filled as soon as you pay for it.

Those are a few of the top reasons why electronic novels are displacing paperbacks for many an avid reader. As always, Ellora's Cave and Cerridwen Press welcomes your questions and comments. We invite you to email us at service@ellorascave.com, service@cerridwenpress.com or write to us directly at: 1056 Home Ave. Akron OH 44310-3502.

NEED A MORE EXCITING
WAY TO PLAN YOUR DAY?

ELLORA'S
CAVEMEN
2006 CALENDAR

COMING THIS FALL

THE ELLORA'S CAVE LIBRARY

Stay up to date with Ellora's Cave Titles in Print with our Quarterly Catalog.

To recieve a catalog,
send an email with your name
and mailing address to:
CATALOG@ELLORASCAVE.COM
or send a letter or postcard
with your mailing address to:
Catalog Request
c/o Ellora's Cave Publishing, Inc.
1337 Commerce Drive #13
Stow, OH 44224

COMING TO A BOOKSTORE NEAR YOU!

ELLORA'S CAVE
2005

BEST SELLING AUTHORS TOUR

Lady Jaided

The premier magazine for today's sensual woman

Lady Jaided magazine is devoted to exploring the sexuality and sensuality of women. While there are many similarities between the sexual experiences of men and women, there are just as many if not more differences. Our focus is on the female experience and on giving voice and credence to it. Lady Jaided will include everything from trends, politics, science and history to gossip, humor and celebrity interviews, but our focus will remain on female sexuality and sensuality.

A Sneak Peek at Upcoming Stories

Clan of the Cave Woman
Women's sexuality throughout history.

The Sarandon Syndrome
What's behind the attraction between older women and younger men.

The Last Taboo
Why some women – even feminists – have bondage fantasies

Girls' Eyes for Queer Guys
An in-depth look at the attraction between straight women and gay men

Available Spring 2005

www.LadyJaided.com

Lady Jaided Regular Features

Jaid's Tirade
Jaid Black's erotic romance novels sell throughout the world, and her publishing company Ellora's Cave is one of the largest and most successful e-book publishers in the world. What is less well known about Jaid Black, a.k.a. Tina Engler is her long record as a political activist. Whether she's discussing sex or politics (or both), expect to see her get up on her soapbox and do what she does best: offend the greedy, the holier-than-thous, and the apathetic! Don't miss out on her monthly column.

Devilish Dot's G-Spot
Married to the same man for 20 years, Dorothy Araiza still basks in a sex life to be envied. What Dot loves just as much as achieving the Big O is helping other women realize their full sexual potential. Dot gives talks and advice on everything from which sex toys to buy (or not to buy) to which positions give you the best climax.

On the Road with Lady K
Publisher, author, world traveler and Lady of Barrow, Kathryn Falk shares insider information on the most romantic places in the world.

Kandidly Kay
This Lois Lane cum Dave Barry is a domestic goddess by day and a hard-hitting sexual deviancy reporter by night. Adored for her stunning wit and knack for delivering one-liners, this Rodney Dangerfield of reporting will leave no stone unturned in her search for the bizarre truth.

A Model World
CJ Hollenbach returns to his roots. The blond heartthrob from Ohio has twice been seen in Playgirl magazine and countless other publications. He has appeared on several national TV shows including The Jerry Springer Show (God help him!) and has been interviewed for Entertainment Tonight, CNN and The Today Show. He has been involved in the romance industry for the past 12 years, appearing on dozens of romance novel covers and calendars. CJ's specialty is personal interviews, in which people have a tendency to tell him everything.

Hot Mama Cooks
Sex is her food, and food is her sex. Hot Mama gives aphrodisiac a whole new meaning. Join her every month for her latest sensual adventure -- with bonus recipe!

Empress on the Mount
Brash, outrageous, and undeniably irreverent, this advice columnist from down under will either leave you in stitches or recovering from hang-jaw as you gawk at her answers to reader questions on relationships and life.

Erotic Fiction from Ellora's Cave
The debut issue will feature part one of "Ferocious," a three-part erotic serial written especially for Lady Jaided by the popular Sherri L. King.

ELLORA'S CAVE
ROMANTICA PUBLISHING

Discover for yourself why readers can't get enough of the multiple award-winning publisher Ellora's Cave. Whether you prefer e-books or paperbacks, be sure to visit EC on the web at www.ellorascave.com for an erotic reading experience that will leave you breathless.

www.ellorascave.com